Death on the Rocks

DEATH ON THE ROCKS

A Lucy Trimble Mystery

Eric Wright

A Castle Street Mystery

THE DUNDURN GROUP
TORONTO · OXFORD

Copy-editor: Jennifer Bergeron
Design: Jennifer Scott
Printer: Transcontinental

Canadian Cataloguing in Publication Data

Wright, Eric
    Death on the rocks: a Lucy Trimble mystery

1ˢᵗ Canadian ed.
(A Castle Street mystery)
ISBN 1-55002-381-0

I. Title. II. Series: Castle Street mystery.

PS8595.R58D43 2002   C813'.54   C2002-901072-1   PR9199.3.W66D48 2002

1   2   3   4   5   06   05   04   03   02

THE CANADA COUNCIL | LE CONSEIL DES ARTS
FOR THE ARTS | DU CANADA
SINCE 1957 | DEPUIS 1957

Canada

ONTARIO ARTS COUNCIL
CONSEIL DES ARTS DE L'ONTARIO

We acknowledge the support of the **Canada Council for the Arts** and the **Ontario Arts Council** for our publishing program. We also acknowledge the financial support of the **Government of Canada** through the **Book Publishing Industry Development Program, The Association for the Export of Canadian Books**, and the **Government of Ontario** through the **Ontario Book Publishers Tax Credit** program.

Care has been taken to trace the ownership of copyright material used in this book. The author and the publisher welcome any information enabling them to rectify any references or credit in subsequent editions.

J. Kirk Howard, President

Printed and bound in Canada.
Printed on recycled paper.

Dundurn Press
8 Market Street
Suite 200
Toronto, Ontario, Canada
M5E 1M6

Dundurn Press
73 Lime Walk
Headington, Oxford,
England
OX3 7AD

Dundurn Press
2250 Military Road
Tonawanda NY
U.S.A. 14150

Death on the Rocks

Chapter One

At seven-thirty on Tuesday morning, Lucy Trimble lay awake beside her racehorse-trainer lover in the bedroom of his farmhouse. They usually slept here only on weekends, but if Johnny did not have to be early at the track, they sometimes commuted for one more day if the weather was good.

Her bottom and thighs still ached from the horse riding Sunday afternoon (he was teaching her to canter), and she would feel it more when she moved — pleasant pain, yet still pain enough to make her hesitate to embrace the moment of getting up. But she had a forty-five minute drive to her office on Queen Street, where she would wait for the phone call to tell her she was needed, and then it was a twenty-minute drive to the trade show at the Coliseum on the Lakeshore where she would meet her client. Time to start the day.

Beside her, Johnny grunted, stirred, farted quietly, and explored the bed behind him with his foot. Lucy tried to calculate if she had time to make love as well as wash, dress, and eat breakfast. Not really. Not properly. She reached out on her side of the bed until her foot found the edge, then downwards until she touched the rug, sliding her body the necessary inch or so across the bed. She rolled fully onto her side, trying to move without disturbing the duvet and so create a current of air, and edged the other foot out and onto the floor, then braced herself to slide out gently, silently. She stood up to shuck off her night-dress and felt Johnny's hand.

"Where are you going?"

"Work. I didn't want to disturb you."

"Not disturbed. Very calm."

"You'll have to be quick. I have to be in Toronto by nine-thirty."

Comstock was always at his fondest in the morning. Lucy liked to think that what she got then was the pure Johnny, bursting with love for her: he awoke, he saw, he adored. The fact that it might just be physiological didn't matter.

She slid back under the duvet, gave him a long unfocussed hug, then arranged herself to receive him. He failed to move to her.

"Not interested?" she asked.

"Stop looking at your watch."

"I do have to go soon."

"So you said. Come back when you have more time." He turned away, scrunching down into the bed, closing his eyes.

Lucy thought, this is getting fraught, and I don't know why. She thought of the Trog, Johnny's imme-diate and only predecessor: in the same situation, he would have jumped her in a trice and been asleep again before she had properly got out of bed. That would have been that. Or not woken up. Or got up and made her breakfast. In any event, he would not have been offended just because she looked at her watch. And then she saw which way her thoughts were going and clamped her mind shut. The idea of comparing Johnny with bald, big-nosed, gap-toothed Ben, which she was just about to do, was absurd.

She moved smartly now, showering briefly without washing her hair, donning a summer dress and grabbing a sweater in case the Coliseum was air-conditioned, then breakfast — a glass of orange juice half full of bran, a slice of toast and honey, a cup of tea. By eight-thirty she was on Highway 404, reflecting on the changes in her circumstances in the past year and a half.

A year ago she had arrived in Toronto, a forty-nine-year-old part-time library worker and the owner of a bed-and-breakfast establishment in Longborough, a town a hundred and fifty kilometres east of Toronto. Two years before that she had disentangled herself from a dominating husband and taken flight, literally (from him) and metaphorically into a freedom that was still testing her. She had met the first challenge by saying yes to the overtures of the Trog, a guest of the bed-and-breakfast establishment. Even then she knew that it wasn't the Trog that she was saying yes to, but the possibility of a new world, and soon the death of a cousin created the opportunity to say goodbye to the Trog and to Longborough and move to Toronto. There, very soon after she arrived, Lucy met Johnny Comstock, the Lancelot of Woodbine racetrack, and knew that she had made the right move.

She had thought until now that there need be no ending to their relationship, but this morning, driving down Highway 404, she was troubled by a doubt. It seemed to her that there was something less than spontaneous about Johnny's reaction that morning, as if he was not so much offended, but finding an excuse to take offence. But why? Why was it wrong of her to check the time? The world's work had to go on, no matter who was feeling horny, didn't it? Not enough time? They would have had enough time if he had really wanted her.

· The traffic slowed to a dawdle, and then it stopped. Half a mile away, a truck loaded with water-melons had overturned as it hit a car coming off the ramp from Major Mackenzie Drive, temporarily blocking all three lanes. Lucy had forgotten to bring her cell phone with her, and by the time the blockage cleared, she was anxious about getting to her office before Greta called. Already the morning's tiny piece of grit was sinking to the bottom of her mind, its sharp edges coated with the first forgetting skin.

The greengrocer on the corner of Queen and Egerton was open, and the bread-and-milk store, but the restaurants were still closed except for one Por-tuguese café where Lucy bought herself some coffee to take up to her office. None of the other tenants of the second floor — the chiropodist, the speech thera-pist or the chiropractor — were working, but her landlord, Peter Tse, was in his office, talking on the telephone with the door open. Lucy unlocked the door of her own office, guessing who Peter was talk-ing to, and looked across Queen Street to see if Nina, her travel agent friend, was also talking on the phone, but her office was dark. Peter Tse owned Nina's building as well as Lucy's, and Lucy had not been able to make up her mind if Nina was his mistress.

"What you workin' on today, Lucy?" Peter said from behind her, making her jump.

"Crime never sleeps," she said. "You look spiffy." Peter was handsome and athletically trim and he was wearing what she thought of as his betting costume — grey cotton trousers, a cream linen jacket, and a white shirt open at the neck — the clothes he wore to go to the racetrack. She looked at her watch, "Bit early for Woodbine?"

"They're at Fort Erie this week. I'm taking my niece to Niagara Falls," Peter said. "Wanna come?" Peter was one of three brothers, only one of whom was married with an eight-year-old daughter, so the two unmarried brothers had to share a single niece. Peter got to take her to school in the mornings, and for an outing about once a month.

"I'm working. Enjoy yourself."

"'Ow about you? Not going down to Fort Erie? Comstock's got a runner in the big race."

"Johnny's going, of course," she said. But it was a flustered remark; of course he would be going to watch his own horse in the big race, but she was caught not even remembering that there was a big race that day. Was that why he was offended?

Peter was watching her face. "Did'jer forget? Nemmind; 'e'll have a lot to think about."

"He won't miss me, you mean?"

"I guess. You're late. Your phone's been ringing already. Some Golden woman." Peter had a key to her office, and when she was out he answered her phone in the guise of her assistant, a role he enjoyed. Lucy felt the idea of an assistant gave her some heft. As he spoke, the phone rang again. She turned to answer it and waved him goodbye, then swung in her chair to watch out of the window to see if he crossed over to Nina's block.

"Who answered your phone?" Greta Golden asked. "Someone with a cockney accent. Said he was your assistant."

"That was my landlord. You saw him yesterday."

"But he's Chinese, isn't he? The one I saw?"

"He's a Chinese cockney. I'll explain sometime, but that's all it is. He's Chinese and he's got a cockney accent. He grew up in Soho, he told me, but he might have been teasing me. He often does."

When no more was forthcoming, Greta said, "All right, then. *My* admirer has arrived. Come to the booth and I'll show him to you. Bring your handcuffs."

Chapter Two

She had met Greta Golden on the stairs when she arrived at her office the morning before, and the two of them had climbed silently to the second floor together, unaware that they had a common destination. At the door of Lucy's office, the woman stopped as Lucy fumbled for her keys.

"Are you the — er — detective?" she asked.

"Lucy Trimble," she agreed. "What can I do for you? Wait a minute. Let's get inside and sit down. Sorry."

The woman was about forty, at least six feet tall with a thin, handsome face that became pretty when she smiled and with an amused twist to her mouth which suggested that she was perfectly aware that everyone she met wondered, at first, what it was like to be that tall. A knowing face, Lucy thought.

In the office the woman waited for Lucy to get settled, then began, "Someone is trying to find out things about me, and I want to know who he is and what he is trying to find out."

Now there's a classic opening, Lucy thought. "How? I mean how do you know he's trying to find out about you? Who told you?"

"He's appeared where I work, and asked at least three people questions about me, and they've told me."

"Where is that? Where you work."

"I'm a wholesaler and retailer of pottery, mainly native crafts. I have a store on Davenport, The Good Earth, but most of my business is selling to the trade."

"Has he approached you?"

"I haven't actually seen him myself. He usually pops up when I've left the scene. I've had the feeling that if I look round quickly, I'll see him, but you can't keep whirling round in public, as if you're playing 'What's the time Mr. Wolf?', can you?" She leaned forward in her chair, bringing her knees together, hooked her feet over the rung of her chair and put her arms round her knees.

Lucy, looking at her stork-like legs, thought, that's what you do when you're that tall. Either you try to tuck the extra inches out of sight gracefully, or you flaunt them. Greta didn't care who thought she was too long in the leg. "And you'd like me to find out who he is?" Lucy asked.

"And what he wants. And make him bugger off."

Lucy took a small chance. "An admirer?"

"A what?" The woman leaned forward. "An admirer? What are we talking about? I've had my share of admirers, sure — well, nearly my share — but I've never had a worshipper from afar. You mean like a ... pop star? Someone besotted with me? I think not. You have to know me to appreciate me."

"You can't think of a time someone has behaved strangely lately — you know like staring at you from across the room, or ... you've been ... er ... polite to who might have ... you know?" Lucy was trying not to used the word "encouraged," but as she asked the question she was noting that the woman's costume — old bell-bottom slacks, a shirt, and a hip-length coat of jean material — her working costume, no doubt — was hardly provocative.

The woman smiled at Lucy's struggle to find the right word. "I *think* I know what you mean," she said, her tone playfully echoing what seemed like Lucy's diffidence. "Some stranger who gets a hard-on at the mere sight of me, you mean; someone I've unintentionally given the wrong signals to? No. I travel a lot, alone, and I think you could say that I am more than ordinarily careful about who I come on to. Anyway, I'm not the right shape for perverts, am I?" She passed a hand lightly over her nearly flat chest and looked down at herself, grinning.

"How long has this been going on?"

"At least two days, probably three. What I mean is, suddenly, in the last two days he's approached these people at the trade show that's on now, so he probably started before that, finding out where I would be now."

"This is a new one for me," Lucy said, after she had absorbed this. "I suppose we do have to consider the possibility that he's out of control, maybe dangerous."

"You mean he might try to attack me? Ah, come on. Maybe he's a maniac, but surely it's more likely ... oh hell, I don't know why he's interested in me.

Maybe he mistakes me for someone he once knew. A big girl in Grade Three."

The phone rang and Lucy answered it. "Yes," she said. "I'll call you back." It was her landlord asking her if she wanted him to fetch her some coffee. She moved some papers around, found her desk diary and made an entry, then made a notation on her calendar. She believed or she had read somewhere that these first few minutes of an interview were important in creating the right impression on a prospective client — one of efficiency and busyness, of someone who is dealing with several other problems while she is listening to this client. Thus she had agreed when Peter suggested that he phone her whenever she had someone in the office, to contribute to the effect, but now, after a year, it felt slightly silly. The note she made to herself was to tell her landlord she could manage without the call in future. "Have you made any enemies recently? Professional ones?"

"You mean like upsetting a business competitor? I've wondered about that, but I haven't done anything I know of."

"No disputes with your customers?"

"There *was* one, a retailer, who tried to claim compensation because she twisted her ankle on our back stairs. I had a warehouse sale and she was carrying some merchandise to her car."

"Are the stairs dangerous?"

"Not in the least, but she didn't leave a hand free for either of the two perfectly good hand-rails. She claimed my steps were too narrow."

"Did she sue you for damages?"

"She wanted her medical bills and three months' pay for the time she was off work. I was going to offer to pay her medical bills but my lawyer said, no, that was tantamount to admitting the steps were dangerous, and anybody else who fell down in the future could claim. So she sued me and we wound up in court. She lost, and had to pay my costs as well as her own." She paused.

"Did you hear from her again?"

"A couple of nights later someone broke all four big windows of my warehouse, throwing rocks. Kids, the police said, because they didn't take anything. I thought it might be her, until the police caught the kids. See how easy it is to get paranoid?"

"But this is a man, you say."

"That's what I hear."

"Did your friends tell you what he looks like?"

Greta pulled a slip of paper from her jacket pocket. "I collated their descriptions." She cleared her throat, like a lecturer. "Medium height, middle-aged, but *young* middle-aged — I wonder if someone is saying that about me? — black crinkly hair parted high up, handsome, one said, more sort of nice-looking, another said, sort of solid-looking, the third one said, has a 'wide face' — that's interesting, isn't it? Not too many wide faces about — she's from Wales: probably she means 'broad' — formally dressed with a tie and suit, but not too stylish, thick through the chest, good teeth, but fan-shaped, slightly outdoorsy complexion." She finished, grinning. "Good, isn't it?" She held out the piece of paper for Lucy.

"It's a start." They looked at each other for a few moments.

"Could he be a spy?" Lucy asked. "No, no, I don't mean a John Le Carré type, but there are commercial spies, aren't there? People who try to find out what you are doing. Is the business doing well?"

"Yes, it is. Very well. There have been a couple of stories about me, one in the *Globe* and another in a magazine, and I've been feeling my neck a bit lately because of that. I suppose it's possible that this guy is trying to get an idea of how I run my business. I don't know. At any rate, let's find out. I must say you're full of ideas. Will you take me on?"

"You know my fee?"

"Fifty an hour, minimum four hours, right? What about the maximum?"

"A thousand a day for working round the clock, which never happens. How did you know the fee?"

"I heard, from Nina Sobczyk."

"Ah." Lucy felt slightly deflated, having hoped that she had developed a small reputation that had rippled out beyond that area of Queen Street.

"It was your name that got me, though: Lucy Trimble, sort of reminded me of ..." the woman stopped, keeping her amusement at bay, but not abandonning it entirely.

"Like Nancy Drew," Lucy said. "I know. Maybe I did it unconsciously. But there it is. I should change it."

"Oh, no. But you should advertise, shouldn't you, at least in the Yellow Pages? As I told Nina, there isn't a single woman detective or investigator listed there. I looked because I thought another woman might be more likely to know if this admirer of mine is some kind of creep. Then Nina told me about you. Does it sound like your kind of job?"

And now Lucy thought she heard behind the words a familiar note, the tinge of doubt about Lucy's fitness for the job, even though Nina had vouched for her. By "another woman" Greta Golden meant someone who could handle (and had been handled by) the Toronto male animal, not one who, after a year in the city, still looked like a fifty-year-old Daughter of the Empire in from the country to see *The Phantom of the Opera*. Nina said it was a spic-and-span look, a shiningness, that marked her out from the Toronto scene.

Lucy swung round to face her computer. "Let me open a file. Name?"

"Greta Golden."

"Address?"

The woman gave her home address on Price Street, and a business address on Spadina. "My warehouse," she added.

"That's just down the block."

"That's why Nina is my travel agent."

"Right. Task, then: To identify — what shall we call him — nuisance follower?"

"That sounds about right."

Lucy swung back. "Can you give me a list of all the people who have mentioned him to you?"

"There are only the three I told you about."

"They all live in the city?"

"No. One of them does. One lives in Hamilton, and one in Ottawa."

Lucy frowned. "I don't understand. This character has travelled to Hamilton and Ottawa just to ask about you?"

"Let me explain. All of us have been attending a trade show here in Toronto. You know? A gift show?

I have a booth there, where I meet my customers, the retailers. These two other wholesalers told me about this man watching me, as well as one of my customers.

"How long does the show go on?"

"Until Thursday."

"When did it start?"

"Sunday. Yesterday."

"And all this happened yesterday?"

"No. See, the wholesalers who are displaying their stuff got in last Thursday to set up their booths and the displays, and no one is really checking on who is coming and going before the show officially opens, so he could have been there for a few days, watching. He was certainly around on Saturday."

"Is he still around?"

"I haven't been in yet. That's why I'm dressed like this. The reps are looking after the booth, and I planned to spend the day walking the show, checking out the competition."

Lucy sat back. "Maybe we should wait. You're bound to catch a glimpse of him sometime if he really is following you about, and we could take it from there. You might recognize him."

The woman waved Lucy's suggestion away. "I might not see him but the others have promised to tell me if *they* do. Can you come out to the show tomorrow? All three of the people who've seen him will be there then. I'll make some phone calls and tell them you'll be by."

"These people sell pottery, too?"

"Veronica Prokaschka, from Hamilton, sells glass she imports from eastern Europe, mostly the Czech Republic. The Ottawa lady, Mrs Anastokas, sells Indian stuff that she buys locally, near Ottawa — moccasins, those beaded capotes, you know. This is a gift show."

"And the third?"

"May Tercil. She owns a store on Bloor Street near Bathurst. I've sold to her for years."

Lucy looked back at the screen. "Any other ideas yourself?"

"We've just been over that, haven't we?"

"Do you feel frightened?"

"Not especially. More curious. Well, a little bit, yes. Call it a frisson. That's why I'm here."

"You live alone?"

"No." She paused to find the right beginning to her next sentence. "Leonard's a photographer, an industrial photographer. We've been together for four years and not a cross word spoken. *He* isn't having me watched. He doesn't have any serious enemies or jilted lovers, either. He thinks I'm being a little silly. His idea is that the tax department has read that little piece in the *Globe* and is trying to get a fix on my rich lifestyle. Do they do that? I mean, chase down rumours about people's incomes? Anyway, he suggested I come to you — well, someone like you. He was sort of telling me to see a doctor and stop bothering him. I think he has the idea that you will tell me to forget it."

"That's my first response. You've got an admirer, or someone who thinks he knows you from somewhere but is too shy to approach until he makes sure. But we can make sure. I'll keep the next three days clear, but I won't come out unless I'm needed. Call me at the first sight of him. I'll start the clock then. If I get any other big offers, I'll let you know; otherwise I'll send you a token bill for giving you priority."

"Fair enough." Greta turned her head sideways and Lucy saw the the classic outline of her face, like a design on one of her own imported vases. Perhaps that's what her admirer saw, Lucy thought. It was probably what had got her the photographer.

"What time will you be here tomorrow?" Greta asked.

"What time do the doors open at the show?"

"Ten."

"I'll be here in the office then, waiting for your call. But if you find someone lurking in the bushes when you wake up in the morning, I have a cell phone. Is there a telephone in your — what? — stall?"

"Booth. Here." The woman pulled out a card. "The phone number of the booth is on the back."

Lucy took one of her own cards from a little rack on her desk and wrote the number of her cell phone. She said, "Does the business belong solely to you?"

"Yes. It was my mother's. She started it in the late fifties, just a little basement shop on Cumberland, but when the flower children moved in she saw that she belonged up on Davenport where the interior decorators were starting to open up. She had terrific business instincts, did Ma."

"Was she a potter, herself?"

Greta laughed. "She told me once she was the only person she knew in the sixties who wasn't a potter, or tie-dyer, or basket-weaver. It was the times: the big word was 'creative' and everyone tried to find something to be creative with, or about. What Ma did was sell the stuff. She bought the best of them — she had a good eye, even if she couldn't turn a wheel herself

— and that was what she thought she could be doing, run a sort of Canadian crafts shop.

"But then the people selling Eskimo art on Bloor Street started to compete with her by taking on some of her lines, and the Canadian Guild of Potters opened their own shop, and there was the Crafts Guild, so Ma stopped thinking Canadian exclusively and went looking for native pottery wherever it could be found cheap and kept exclusive. I think she started by importing stuff from Mexico, but she soon went a lot farther afield.

"I took over when she was killed, three years ago. I had been working with Ma for some time, so I had no problems keeping going. I'm doing okay."

"Was it an accident?"

"Ma? Sort of. She was shot by a burglar in her Florida motel room. She just happened to be in his way."

"And ... your father?"

"He died when I was born. Another accident. I'm the only child they had." Greta clearly felt that they were wandering off topic. "That all you need?" she asked.

Lucy nodded. "I'll wait to hear from you tomorrow. I can't think of anything else at the moment."

The woman stood and looked around the room. "It *is* a bit like the stories," she said.

Lucy waited for more.

"You know, the ones where the private eye has a ratty little office, is behind with his rent, keeps a bottle of bourbon in one drawer and a gat in the other. Sorry. It's not *really* ratty here. It's just what you think as you come up the stairs. And I doubt if you have any bourbon."

"Or a gat."

"Right. I'm just making it up, aren't I? Lucy Trimble, Private Eye. But what's the mirror for?" She nodded towards a huge free-standing mirror near the back wall. "Sam Spade didn't have one of those."

"I use it to check my costume. I use a lot of disguises."

"Really? Wow!"

"No, *not* really. I was joking. I inherited the mirror along with the agency when my cousin died. Ask Nina what he used it for. She knows."

"I remember. She told me. He used to watch Nina in it. Is that true? Is it possible?"

"Hold on. Stand over there." Lucy picked up the phone. "Nina," she said, when she was connected. "You have a friend here who wants to see the mirror working. Greta. Greta Golden. Stand in your window, would you?" She put the phone down. To Greta Golden, she said, "See?"

"Well, there she is. She's waving. Can she see me if I wave back? Ah, she's gone."

"She's probably got a client. So I'll be here tomorrow waiting for your call, Ms. Golden."

"Greta. Nice to meet you. Lucy. Do you mind?"

Lucy shook her head. "It's easier. That is, until you want to complain about my bill."

"Don't worry, I could call you darling and still beat you down."

"You really have no idea why this character could be following you around?"

"Not the slightest."

"Are you curious about him? Personally?"

"You mean in case he's filthy rich, or something? I told you, I'm happily unmarried."

"Good."

"It's a thought, though, isn't it? Leonard can't even pay his share of the rent. But, no. I just want to know why he's there."

Chapter Three

As the woman's steps descended the stairs, her landlord put his head round the door. "Paying customer?" he asked.

"I think so. Nina recommended me."

"Never mind 'oo recommended you. Did you get anythink on account?" He rubbed his thumb and forefinger together.

"No, dammit. I forgot. Listen. She's coming back. Quick. Bug off."

Greta appeared in the doorway. "You didn't tell me how you want to be paid," she said.

"I'll need a deposit when I agree to take you on," Lucy said. "If he doesn't turn up again, you won't need me. But you can give me fifty now, which I'll keep if you don't need me."

Greta approached the desk and made out a cheque. Lucy put it in a drawer. "Tomorrow then," she said. "Ten o'clock."

Greta's steps descended the stairs once more and Peter Tse reappeared. "That was clever, Loosie," he said.

"Were you listening?"

"I was checking the smoke alarm in the corridor. *Now* would you like that coffee?"

"My turn." Lucy tried to flip a two-dollar coin over the desk but it landed in her "in" tray. Peter took it and disappeared.

"Who was she?" he asked when he returned with the coffee, and sat down down the client's chair. "What did she want?"

"She thinks she's being followed."

"Yeah? Be easy to spot in a crowd, wouldn't she? How did she hear about you?"

"I told you. Nina."

"Ah, right." Tse sipped his coffee. "Did you talk to Nina yet?"

"No."

"She's in now. I just took her some coffee. You could give her a ring now."

Lucy said nothing. From the beginning of her tenancy in his building, when she had arrived to find her dead cousin's office broken into and the contents trashed, Peter Tse had looked out for her, assuming her need for a bit of protection in the Toronto jungle. He had been very useful when her husband had appeared in her office one day, threatening her, and he had escorted her to the races once when she was on a case, and on the whole she was grateful for his proximity and availability, but she was beginning to feel the need to push him back a little, a desire to start to manage on her own.

Peter got the message and stood up. "Before I

leave you to solve the case of the Friendly Female Giant," he said, "I've got another one for you."

Lucy sighed noisily, and waited for the story.

"There's these two hooligans," he said. "Real tearaways. They steal this car, see, and drive it to somewhere quiet so they can strip it before they dump it. So they look in the trunk ..."

"And find a body."

"How did you know?"

"That's what they always find. In the trunk."

"Yeah? This one really happened, in Australia. Anyway, now they've got a problem. They can't go to the filth because they've both got records ..."

"All they have to do is drive it to the nearest parking garage — Yorkville would do — and leave it there. If they've stolen the car, there's nothing to link them to it," Lucy said.

He nodded, surprised at the size of the hole in his plot. "Yeah, right." After a moment he began again, "Then ..."

But before he could re-weave it, she added, "Now I've got to get on with a real case." She looked at her watch and stood up.

"Kicking me out, are you?"

She smiled, and picked up her purse. "And I don't think I need you to phone me anymore when I have a client. I think I can handle myself now."

"You *are* getting to be a big girl, aren't you? How long shall I say you'll be?"

Lucy said, "I have to talk to the owner of a drug store on Queen Street, just a few blocks away. I ought to be back by one, if you want to wait for lunch."

Lucy picked up some toothpaste and a box of Band-Aids and walked down the aisles of the drugstore. It was a narrow store, with products on two walls and on shelves on either side of a central unit. The cash desk was near the door, and the drug-dispensing counter at the back. It was as much corner store as pharmacy, offering, as well as drugs, beauty aids, magazines, paperback novels, candy, biscuits, chutney, toilet paper, household cleaners, a rack of herbal medicines, and a modest range of plain condoms.

She worked her way slowly to the back of the store, observing the help, until she reached the dispensing counter where the pharmacist, Jeffrey Coopman, was waiting for her. He knew who she was, having come to her office with the problem, a tale of money disappearing from the till. Lucy had arranged to visit the store before advising what might be done, and now, under cover of pretending to be explaining a prescription to her, he identified the staff.

Two of the assistants were youngish, cheerful girls; the third was middle-aged, stick-thin and laconic, with bi-focals that she adjusted by wrinkling her nose and throwing her head back when she wanted to read labels. Her virtue seemed to be that she knew everything. "Do we have Spectro-Tar, Nan?" one of the young assistants asked. "On the shelf behind Mr. Coopman." She lowered her head to look across the room. "There's none left, though. I'll reorder." "Ever heard of Prost-Ease, Nan?" the other one asked. "Herbal," Nan said. "But we don't carry it. Buy it at the health food store." She was that kind of assistant.

Apart from these three, a little lady with a complicated hairdo and a lot of makeup, apparently the pharmacist's wife, flitted about in a white coat in a proprietorial way, seeming to specialize in giving advice about cosmetics.

Lucy said, "Do the two girls usually have most to do with the cash register?"

Jeffrey Coopman said, "Nan hates being on cash. She does it only if she has to, during an emergency, maybe twice a week."

"It's difficult for me to watch from the floor," Lucy said. "You can't browse the aspirin rack for long without looking suspicious. What's upstairs, above the cash register?"

"Storage rooms. Used to be an apartment back in the days when you lived over your store."

"Could I put a camera in there?"

"I guess. I thought that's what it would come to." Coopman sighed. He was a tall, loose-jointed man, with grey and brown hair that grew thickly above a face that had the bumps and hollows that might have made his face "craggy," but now was pale and soft, like an outdoorsman who has spent six months in jail. "But I want you to fix it so that I can control it from back here with a button. I'll just do spot checks," he said. "I know the likely times. I did a little skimming myself, once." He smiled, waiting.

"You're supposed to look shocked," he said. "No? Anyway, this guy I was working for when I first graduated used to have a cash register with wooden drawers and a bell that went 'ping!' But if you kept your hand on the bell it didn't go 'ping', so you could open the drawer without him hearing you and lift a couple of tens — he put the twenties in his pocket as soon as he got them."

"I'm not surprised."

"He was overcharging the customers and under-paying me, so I was just evening things up a bit."

"For you, not the customers."

"I did what I could for them by never catching anyone shoplifting. So I know what you're saying. But it's hard to skim when you've got a lineup of customers. I'll make selective spot checks. That way I'll save money on videotape, right?"

Lucy said, "You won't save much."

"That's how I want it set up, though."

"It doesn't make sense," Lucy protested. "If you don't find the thief with these selective spot checks, you'll have to run a continuous tape in the end. Why not do it properly in the first place?"

"We'll do it *my* way first."

Nothing about her previous experience with Coopman had suggested that he was cheap. He had paid her a retainer, in cash, as soon as she had quoted her fee, and the money he would save by inter-rupting the videotape was negligible, so Lucy knew that she wasn't getting the whole story. She decided not to press Coopman. She had said her piece, and if he wanted to ignore her advice, for his own reasons, she would still have earned her fee. But she would keep her wits about her. Coopman, she felt sure, was up to something he wasn't telling her about.

Chapter Four

Now it was Tuesday morning and Peter had met Lucy with the news that someone had been phoning for her. "That woman called Golden," he said.

Lucy just had time to sit down before Greta rang again. "My admirer has arrived," she said. "I'll keep him in my sights until you get here."

Lucy put the phone down and picked up her purse. As she moved to the door, Peter, blocking her way, said, "You remember those two tearaways I told you about?"

"The ones who left the car with the body in the trunk in the parking lot?"

"That's 'em. Well, see, no, the reason they couldn't leave the car in the parking lot was because in the first place they'd taken the car down to the spit of land off Cherry Beach where it's quiet, to strip 'er, see. But when they got there, the filth drew up and asked them if they'd seen anyone come by. These cops were following a citizen who had assaulted someone under the expressway. Now the coppers were friendly enough, but they got a good look at the two villains and at their car so there was no way the two could just leave it in a parking lot and scarper, was there? They'd be picked up in no time, and stuck with the body. Now what?"

"Are they being framed?"

"I think that's what's happening."

"But how would whoever dumped the body know that these two were in the vicinity and about to steal that particular car?"

"I see what you mean. I'll work on it. Anyfing wrong, Lucy?"

"No. Why?"

"You seem a bit out of it. Am I bothering you?"

"Oh, no, Peter. Not you."

"Good. You know, if there *is* something you need ..."

"Just eternal youth."

"In Hong Kong they use the you-know-what of grizzly bears, ground up. Wanna try that?"

"I'll persevere with bran."

"Anyfing wrong?" Lucy asked herself, rehearsing the question. It was one, she realized as soon as Peter asked it, that she had asked a lot lately. Anything wrong? she asked Johnny, as she heard the qualified agreement, the hesitation, the lack of immediate assent (or its opposite, the instant objection) — in short, the pause that was the sign that what she was proposing was flawed in a way he couldn't quickly respond to without offending her. Why? Where was this new uncertainty, this sometimes prickliness, coming from? Why weren't they automatically and continually on the same wavelength still?

There was certainly nothing wrong with the weather yet. She drove down Spadina and turned on to the Lakeshore on her way to the Canadian National Exhibition grounds where the gift show was held. Labour Day had come and gone, marking the transition from summer to fall, but southern Ontario was ignoring the calendar. The trees along the lakeshore were still green (the odd bit of gold, pointing to the fall that was coming, could be dismissed as probably something to do with acid rain), and on the lake a few sailboats were doing their bit to prolong the season. Inside the car there was no need for either the air conditioner or the heater, and when Lucy opened her window an inch, there was still a hint of the scent of newly-cut grass.

Greta had told her to park in the lot closest to the Coliseum, the main exhibition hall, where she had her booth. Driving in though Princes' Gate, Lucy wondered if the Exhibition itself, Ontario's annual fall fair and agricultural show, had changed much. She had not been for more than thirty years, when she had found an excuse to take one last look at it.

Was it still a big deal for kids in small towns, the annual expedition to the Ex, maybe staying overnight with an aunt or big sister who lived in Toronto? The Exhibition was over now, but you could still get a whiff of the animal barns near the Coliseum. She would like to see the horses again. Perhaps next year.

Perhaps. Perhaps it was money? Without having access to his books, she understood Johnny was financially secure, set for life, and he didn't gamble or make risky investments in horseflesh; but he might have suffered a setback she did not know about, mightn't he? Lucy forced herself to speculate objectively. Perhaps he was sick and didn't want to tell her. Not her fault. But she couldn't convince herself. Something was wrong. Something to do with her.

Greta said, "As far as I can tell, he tries to get into conversation with anyone he sees stopping at my booth for long. May Tercil said it started off as if he was trying to pick her up — at ten o'clock in the morning at a trade show! That idea proving absurd upon inspection, she assumed he was just being friendly. Then he zeroed in on the subject of me, she said. Wanted to know all about me. She clammed up, of course, and saved it up to tell me. The other two said much the same, but one of them, Lorna Bentley from Kingston, said he seemed to be signalling that he was interested in getting to know me, but when she offered to introduce him he backed off."

Greta paused to go around to the front of the booth to pick up a catalogue that had slipped onto the floor. As she straightened up, she said, "Jesus, there he is! Don't look round too quickly! He's taken up a position three booths along; he's pretending to look at those cards, but watch him for a minute. It's us he's interested in. When you get close enough, take a look at his badge. See if he's listed in here." She handed Lucy the catalogue of the wholesalers and retailers in attendance. "This will make you look like you have business at the show."

"Do something personal," Lucy said. "Kiss me. On the cheek."

"Do what!"

"Get your diary out. We'll compare diaries. Write something in them, then we kiss. Shows how close we are."

Greta retrieved her diary from the back of the booth, thumbed through it, nodded, wrote something in it, threw the diary in the back, squinted comically at Lucy, then kissed her on the cheek, embraced her fondly, and stood back to look at her face.

"That should do it," Lucy said, shaking herself free and organizing herself to move off. "I'll report back. If you don't see me before, let's have a sandwich at lunchtime. I'll come by at twelve."

"I hope he's not a creep. Well, he *is* a creep, but I hope you can handle him."

"That's my job," Lucy said, simply. "Is he watching me?"

"Yes."

"Good. When I've gone, see if he keeps on watching me. I'll catch your eye from the next booth. You nod if he's watching me, okay?"

Greta did as she was told, in time nodding to Lucy that she now had him all to herself.

He was just as described: fortyish, squarish, wiry black hair, clean-shaven, wearing a grey suit and some kind of school or club tie — dark green with lavender and grey stripes. He carried an olive raincoat, not the grubby fawn kind, thought Lucy, who had recently frightened off an exhibitionist in the classic "flasher's" garment who had been showing his wares in a local cemetery. At this stage it seemed likely that this man was simply taken with Greta Golden, an attractive woman, never mind the height.

As Lucy approached him, he turned away slightly but with some obviousness, and she lingered by the booth to give him a chance to look up naturally.

He glanced at her badge. "A Toronto location?" he asked.

The show was not open to the public and everyone was required to wear a badge, identifying them as buyers or exhibitors. Greta had left a badge for Lucy to pick up at the door, identifying her as a representative of a stationery store called Hello Hello Hello, one of Greta's customers. His own badge said simply, Claycrafts UK.

Lucy remembered that she was in the role of a potential customer, so it was all right for him to accost her." Yes, we have a card shop in West Toronto," she said. "And who is Claycrafts UK?"

"What's that?" He looked down at himself. "Oh, yes. Yes. It's a distributor. Casseroles, vases, anything made of clay." He looked at Lucy's badge. "We sell a few cards, too," he added.

"And you're here to buy, or sell?"

"More just scout around, really. Pick up samples. See what our Canadian cousins are doing."

"Found anything worth making the trip for?"

"Quite a lot, yes. Quite a lot that's *interesting*, I mean. But I don't know if there would be much of a market in Ilford, say, for jokes about the Mounties." He took a postcard from the plastic bag he was carrying, a cartoon of American tourists arriving at the Canadian border in midsummer, their car laden down with skis.

"That's a local joke," Lucy said.

"Yes. I can see that, but I don't think it would mean a lot to the average person in Ilford, would you think? Someone who hasn't travelled much. Or is everyone a world traveller these days?"

"I think even people from Ilford could work it out, don't you? It's not that subtle."

He laughed. "You're probably right." He reached in his pocket for a ballpoint pen and a small notebook. "Now I have to go to work. Don't be alarmed, I'm not actually selling anything this trip, but I want to take back a list of ... possible outlets for our products. Justify my expenses. Do you have a card? I left mine in my briefcase."

Lucy remembered in time how her cards identified her. "Mine are at home," she said. "I forgot them when I changed purses this morning. I'll pick up a few from one of the others later."

"Fair enough. In the meantime, do you sell small clay objects? And if so, can I buy you a coffee while I write down your name and address in my diary? There's a place farther along which has donuts and things. Danish pastries. They've got tables and chairs. I'd like a chat with a potential customer about the trade over here."

Lucy allowed herself to be led along the aisle to a coffee bar, and secured two seats at a little plastic table while he lined up for the coffee and pastry. When they were organized, he pointed to the catalogue in Lucy's hand. "You won't find me in there, I'm afraid. I'm a late registrant."

"I wondered."

"Yes. We just decided at the last minute. See if we could get the jump on the competition. Generally we mostly rely on the — er — English fairs. But we thought we'd take a peek at the stuff here. Will you be going over to Birmingham next time?" He flourished the word "Birmingham" as if to demonstrate how familiar he was with the venues of the gift business.

"I doubt if my boss will send me," she said. Then, unable to resist a bit of interrogation, "We did go last year, but it was hard to find anywhere to stay. Where would you recommend we try, next time, in Birmingham?"

"Stay?"

"Yes."

"Where should you stay," he repeated, "in Birmingham."

"Yes. What would you recommend? Where do you stay yourself?"

"In Birmingham?" He looked satisfactorily at a loss, and Lucy congratulated herself. Clearly, the man had not worked hard enough at his cover. Then he said, "I don't actually stay *in* Birmingham. I like to get away from the show in the evening, so I stay in Stratford, not too far away. Bed-and-breakfast place called the Arden Hotel. You have to book a long way ahead because they're nearly always full; good value for money."

That sounded convincing. The man knew about Stratford, anyway. Lucy tried again. "How does this compare to Birmingham? This is a lot bigger, I would think." She watched him calculating, and wondered where he would place his bet.

He shook his head. "Oh, no. Birmingham could swallow this lot. Much bigger." He looked at her for a sign of agreement, but Lucy had no idea. She had hoped to catch him fumbling.

She tried another tack. "How do you go? To Birmingham, I mean."

"Straight up the M40. I could go home at night but it's a bit of a drive in the morning."

"How long does it take?"

He did some sums in his head. "Couple of hours. I come across the M25 and pick up the M40 at High Wycombe. If there's a bit of fog you can get held up, but apart from that it's a straight run."

"Come across from where?"

"Ilford." He sounded surprised. "You know, where I live."

Lucy saw now that he was totally relaxed, and she could not pursue the subject without at least being tedious, even if he was not suspicious. "That's how you know what people in Ilford like?"

"What?"

"What kind of cards."

"Oh, yes. Yes." He paused. "Yes, about two hours by High Wycombe." He waited for a response, then asked, "How about another coffee?"

Lucy shook her head. "How big are these cups? Twenty ounces. I've had my coffee for the day."

"Me, too." He leaned forward. "You sell anything else than cards? We do a line of novelties. Ashtrays, mugs. You know. You do any of that?"

Lucy had been expecting this, the beginning of the questions that would lead to Greta.

"We don't carry any schlock," she said. "No CN Towers, or Mountie dolls."

"Oh, no, no, no. We don't do any of that. No 'Present from Southend' stuff."

"Souvenirs, you mean?"

"That's it. No. Our ashtrays and mugs are all real pottery, not factory stuff. You carry a bit of proper craft work, do you?"

"Some of our cards reproduce native art. From Costa Rica, places like that, and we do carry a bit of pottery, not a whole line but just to complement our cards." (Listen to me, she wanted to say to someone. I know about as much as he does about the trade, but I'm doing well, aren't I?)

"Of course," he said. "Complete the look."

"What?" Lucy, preening herself, had lost the thread.

"The right stuff in a shop window. Gives the place a look."

Now he was floundering again; she nodded warmly to encourage him.

"Where do you buy your pottery?" he asked. "Who supplies you? I'd like to get a line on the Canadian wholesalers."

"We have several suppliers," she said leafing through the catalogue. She stopped at the entry which described Greta's booth. "This is the best, for my money, anyway. I should warn you that the owner is a very good friend of mine so I'm bound to send business her way. But her stuff *is* good."

"Nothing wrong with helping a friend. Known her long, have you?"

"A few years."

"Through the business?"

"At first, yes."

"Did she start it from scratch?"

Lucy felt their roles being reversed. At any moment soon he would discover that she was a fake, too. "I don't think so," she said. "She took it over from her mother."

"Who retired?"

"Died, I think."

"What about the father?" The question was slightly odd, slightly more pointed than the previous chat. This was something he wanted to know about.

"Dead, too, I believe."

"No siblings?"

"I think she's an only child. That's how she got the business."

His body now made the movements that told Lucy the topic was finished, and he began a new one. "Very interesting what happens to small businesses when the owner goes. Family businesses generally carry on if there's a child interested. These days, though, the children have often moved upwards, become professionals: lawyers, doctors. Especially the Asians. So it's the same as if there's no family; the business just closes down. People think that the goodwill is always worth a lot of money, but it's just as easy to start up in competition as to buy an established business like your friend's. And a lot cheaper. When I come across a small business, I always wonder how long it will last and what will happen when the owner dies. Ever think of that?"

"Not much." Now Lucy thought he was trying to divert any suspicion she might have of his questioning by showing his wide familiarity with commerce generally. "Are you staying for the whole show?"

"I'm hoping to be able to get away tomorrow. Depends."

"On what?"

"If I've ticked everything off. Look, I'm enjoying this. It's a bit lonely sometimes at these things. How about joining me for a snack? Lunch. On my swindle sheet."

"All right. Where? There seem to be a lot of places in this building."

"Not here. Let's go uptown — I mean downtown, don't I? I've seen nothing of Toronto yet. But I forgot. You're supposed to be tramping the floor, aren't you?"

"I'll come in early tomorrow to make up the time. Where, then?"

"You'd know best."

If only that were true. She still felt a stranger in Toronto except around her office at Queen and Egerton, and the little area around Avenue Road and Davenport, near Johnny Comstock's town flat. And the racetrack. And then she remembered where they were and that no one would expect her to be knowledgeable about an area she only visited for trade shows. "I never go out from here," she said. "Ask someone. Find a place. I'll meet you at the Good Earth booth at 12:30. We'll go from there."

"I don't know your name yet," he said.

"That's right. Lucy Trimble."

"Michael," he said. "Michael Curnow. All right then, see you at half-past twelve."

Chapter Five

Lucy opened her catalogue and stayed sitting until he left. She kept him in sight until he turned into a phone booth by the exit doors, then she hurried back and rolled her eyes at Greta to follow her to the ladies' room at the end of the aisle.

"It's eleven o'clock," Lucy said to Greta in the mirror. "Four o'clock in England. Do you have any professional contacts there that you could call and ask a favour of?"

Greta pondered for a few moments. "There's a man in Exeter, in Devon, who's after my body. He runs a little workshop down there where he reproduces Victorian tinware. It's rubbish, but it's made by hand by the locals so it qualifies as native craft, and he's always badgering me to take it. But you won't find it in my catalogue, or him either."

"Call him and ask him if he knows of or can find a pottery company called Claycrafts UK. And if he finds it, have him call the office and ask for Michael Curnow. How well do you know this tin man? Will he go to some trouble for you?"

"Oh, I think so. He's been trying to get his leg over, as the Brits say, for years. Letting him do me a favour will give him hope."

"Call him now, please. In three quarters of an hour it'll be closing time in England."

Curnow was still thumbing through the Yellow Pages. Giving up, he looked at his watch, made a note in a small jotter, and started out on what was evidently to be a time-killing stroll.

Lucy made sure he was well out of sight before she rejoined Greta in the front of the booth, now in the process of trying to connect with her friend in Exeter. She waved Lucy away and spread the fingers of one hand three times to indicate that Lucy should come back in fifteen minutes.

"You don't look like a female private eye," Mary Anastokas, the wholesaler of beaded Indian clothing said.

"What's a female private eye look like?"

"Tough. Ballsy."

"There are several kinds. I'm one of the others. You don't look like an Indian, either, and shouldn't you be called Mary Loon or Annie Littledeer or something like that?"

"If I were an Indian, I think I could have you banned from the show for a remark like that. Actually I'm Welsh, married to a Greek. What about this Michael Curnow who's following Greta?"

"Oh, he's English, I think."

"I can see that. I mean, did you get a fix on him?

"I'm trying to. Did you talk to him?"

"Not really. As soon as it was obvious he was more than casually interested in Greta, I clammed up."

"Did you get any impression of what he wanted?"

"The usual, I would think. Maybe what bothers Greta is that he hasn't come on to her directly. Is she overreacting? I just mentioned that this Englishman seemed to have the hots for her. That was all."

"Others here said the same. It's made her nervous. What's that smell?" She leaned forward and inhaled deeply, then picked up a caribou parka and sniffed.

"That smoky burnt-fat smell is the biggest selling point. The Germans, especially, like its authenticity. Actually I think there's a factory in Yellowknife where they spray it on."

Greta was waiting for her at the booth, triumphant and agitated. "He doesn't exist," she said. "My man in Exeter pushed all the buttons and no one has heard of him or his Claycrafts UK. So what do we have here? Time to call the cops?"

"He doesn't seem dangerous."

"Wait 'til he puts that raincoat on."

"I don't think he's life-threatening. Let me make a phone call. I'm supposed to have lunch with him. I'll come by after lunch."

It was eleven-thirty. Lucy borrowed Greta's cell phone and retired to a corner.

Jack Brighton, private investigator and aspiring stand-up comic, who had guided Lucy's first fumbling steps as a detective, still made himself available when Lucy encountered a new problem which Brighton's experience might help to solve. In return, Lucy helped paper the house whenever Brighton tried out a new routine at Yuk Yuk's.

"I want to find out something about an Englishman," she said. "He's here, posing as a buyer for a pottery wholesaler in England, but the company doesn't exist. I think he's harmless, but he's acting kind of strange. He's been following my client around. We thought he might be infatuated, or maybe a trade spy trying to find out where she gets her merchandise, but now he's looking a bit strange. Actually, he *looks* very ordinary, but ..."

"They all do, those English guys. Then you dig up the basement and find eight corpses and a set of butcher's knives. All the property of a little guy who does one of those cryptic crosswords on his way to work every morning on the subway. It's being ordinary-looking that lets them get the count up to eight before anyone notices."

"Jack, I'm in a hurry. His name is Michael Curnow, and I'm pretty sure he comes from somewhere called Ilford."

"That all you know?"

"Yes."

"I'll call you back in forty-five minutes precisely, at twelve-twenty-seven. Okay?"

Lucy went for a walk and returned in half an hour to wait for the cell phone to ring.

At twelve-twenty-seven the phone rang and Greta handed the instrument to Lucy. "Bingo," Brighton said, and waited to be asked what he meant.

"Have you found out anything?" she asked

"'Deed I have, Lucy. Let me tell you a story. Once upon a time, twenty years ago — I was staying at one of those campgrounds, you know? I was driving through Idaho — I had a camper and I needed a shower and something to plug my frig into, you know? Anyway, there was this asshole in the next parking spot standing by his camper with a microphone in his hand, saying, 'Come in, anyone. Come in, anyone'. Citizens' band radio was new then, Lucy. Long before cell phones. So finally someone comes in and this guy asks him what the traffic's like, and the weather, stuff like that, all a show for our benefit. Cut a long story short, he didn't learn anything because it turned out he was talking to another asshole two parking spaces away, both of them putting on this performance until they looked up and saw each other."

Lucy thought she would go mad. She could feel Michael Curnow coming down the aisle. "What are you saying, Jack? Quick, quick, and don't swear so much."

"That's what I'm saying. Michael Curnow's an investigator, like me. And you, I guess. He works for Curnow Investigations, who, right now, just have an answering machine to pick up their calls. And you're right. In Ilford. On a street called the Cranbrook. I didn't get the number."

"Thanks, Jack."

"Hey ..."

But she had handed the instrument to Greta as Curnow sailed into view round the corner, tacking towards the booth.

"Mr. Curnow, there you are, right on time. I need about ten minutes alone with my boss, do you mind? I have to tell her about some stuff she should be aware of. A competitor. Just a little time alone."

"Just out of earshot," Greta said, nodding at him in friendly fashion. "Trade secrets."

"Fair enough. Yes. But point me towards the facilities."

Greta got it first. "The loo. Right. See the sign? Washrooms."

When he had trotted away, Lucy asked, "How did you know about 'facilities?'"

"I spend a lot of time in England and I pick up languages quickly. Now, who is he?"

"He's a detective. English, as you realized. Checking up on you."

"What for? A business thing? English? I haven't done anything illegal in England. I didn't even go to Birmingham this year."

"There has to be something. He's trying to find out who you are."

"Tell him. I'm not a bloody imposter. I'm Greta Golden."

Lucy said, "I'd like to lead him on a bit, see if I can get him to talk. Trouble is, I don't know anything about you."

"Make it up." Greta was grinning now. "No, better tell him the truth in case he's already picked up some of it. Here, write this down. I was born in England in 1958. My mother went over for a holiday at the end of her pregnancy with me and got caught short. My father died just after I was born. Got that? I grew up here in Toronto. How are you doing? Went to Queen's University. I always worked for my mother during vacations and then full-time, and I took over the business when she was killed in Florida. Quick, he's coming back. Only child. Never married. Here he is now. Hi there!" She waved at Curnow approaching. Then, quickly, to Lucy," No enemies that I know of. Here he comes."

Lucy turned, waved in turn, said quietly to Greta, "I'm going to tell him I know what he is," and moved towards Curnow.

Greta's mouth hung open, then, as the couple walked off, she called out, "Bring me back the menu. I want to read it over my knitting tonight."

Chapter Six

"What did she mean by that?" Curnow asked.

"She probably thinks you're taking me somewhere grand. Are you?"

"A trendy-looking cove in one of the booths said we ought to go to the Doomsday Tavern on King Street West." He paused to see if she knew the restaurant. "Doesn't sound very appetizing, does it?" he continued, when she failed to react. "He was quite firm, though. Said we'd need a taxi. Where can we get one?"

"I've got a car."

"Have you? Here? Well, then. Where's King Street?"

"I can find my way."

She led them out to the parking lot and they drove north until they came to King and then turned right, watching for the number of the restaurant, which, when they found it, turned out to be one of a strip of restaurants a few blocks west of the electric circus that advertised the theatres and eating palaces of the

Mirvish empire. They found a parking meter almost opposite the restaurant. Lucy parked, put in a loonie, and said, "We've got an hour."

"What happens then?"

"I expect they tow you away. I've never found a parking space in this area before."

"This is grand, for me." Lucy looked round and picked up the menu. "I generally just have a toasted bagel and tea for lunch. Here, listen. 'Two pieces of freshly caught halibut, flash frozen at sea and dipped in our special lite batter made with four secret ingredients and deep-fried to crispy perfection with a heaping order of Yukon Gold french fries with our own mayonnaise for dipping and a side order of made-freshly-for-you cole slaw.' I'll have that."

"It'll be a disappointment after all that rubbish. Anyway, fish and chips is no good over here. No good at home, either, for that matter."

"In England?"

"In Ilford. I only know one place in London, near Russell Square Station, where they still know how to make proper fish and chips. I'll tell you the name if you'll promise not to tell everyone in the gift trade and spoil it. Hullo. Liver and bacon. Surprised to see that here." He called over the waiter, a lanky youth with the cap-and-bells look of someone who liked his job but found it slightly absurd. "What kind of liver is it?"

"Dark red," the youth said. "Not chicken liver." He was quite serious.

"I don't want pork liver. Find out, would you?"

The youth returned immediately. "Baby beef, sir."

"Calves' liver, then?"

A man at the next table caught his attention and shook his head. "Ox," he said.

"I'll have it, anyway. No I won't, I'll have shepherd's pie."

"Good choice, sir." He smiled first at Lucy, then at Curnow.

"How do you know what's good and what isn't?" Curnow asked in an interested tone. "You tried 'em all today?"

"It's all excellent," he said, "You can't go wrong here."

"So whatever I order, you say, 'excellent choice', right?"

"That's right, sir."

"They learn it in catering school," Curnow said to Lucy. "Not how to cook, but how to talk like this."

"And the lady?" the waiter asked.

"Fish and chips and tea," Lucy said.

"And you, sir? To drink? Glass of our specially chosen burgundy?"

"I'll have whatever local beer you've got on tap." Curnow turned to Lucy. "I've been listening, picking up the lingo. People say that here."

"Heineken, is it, sir?"

"That's *local*? I always understood it was Dutch. Or German."

"It's brewed locally to Canadian tastes."

"So what's the point?"

"If you prefer imported, we have it in bottles."

"What? Have what?"

"Heineken." Now the waiter started to giggle.

Curnow looked at Lucy, who said, "Do you make a fuss like this every time?"

"I don't think I'm making a fuss. You would know it if I was. But I don't like being talked to in advertising lingo and PR speak instead of English. 'Brewed locally to Canadian tastes.' What does that mean? German beer for people who don't like German beer? Oh, all right, I give in. I'll have half a pint of whatever comes out of your tap."

The drinks arrived, and almost as quickly the food arrived as the waiter worked to get them out in time for another sitting. They talked of the weather, which was warmer than it had been in England the day before, and of Toronto, which Curnow had never visited before, and of business, and Lucy amused herself watching him make up answers to her questions about the operations of Claycrafts. She was impressed by the skill with which he had turned a morning at the trade show and probably half an hour with the catalogue into a plausible acquaintance with the industry, given that she did not know enough to ask the really difficult questions, about brokerage and warehousing and such. Soon enough Greta's name came into the conversation and Lucy waited for the interrogation to start. But Curnow seemed much less interested in Greta than he had been an hour beforehand. And then, abruptly, he said, "Did I pass?"

"Pass? Pass what?"

"Your little test. You were testing me. See if I could manage my cover. Sorry. Silly word. I mean my false identity. You know who I am, don't you?"

"I know *what* you are, yes."

"I thought so. Not very good at this, am I? I mean the undercover lark. I never pretended to be. It's not my thing. I don't do much of it. But I had to have a story to get into the show, and to find out what I could."

"About Greta Golden? Or The Good Earth?"

"About her. Yes. About her. My turn now. Did she hire you?"

"Hire *me*? Of course not. She just got suspicious of all the clumsy questions and told me, so I got a man I know to check you out. Curnow Investigations, of Ilford." She sat back, waiting.

Curnow consulted a notebook he drew from the pocket of his raincoat. "Lucy Trimble, Private Investigator," he said, adding, "Snap."

"How did you know?"

"You're in the book. I phoned your office, got your assistant."

"Why did you do that?"

"It was the clumsy way you let yourself be picked up by me, like a tart in Soho. I wondered at first if you *were* a tart working the show ..."

"At my age? And at ten o'clock in the morning?"

"Don't knock it. Your age. There's a lot of lonely travellers looking for someone their own age. And the morning's not a bad time. You set all *my* antennae vibrating. But I gave Hello Hello Hello a ring and learned all about you."

"But Angela was in on it. Why didn't she cover for me?"

"I didn't ask Angela, who I assume is the owner and is therefore at the show. I asked her assistant who is minding the shop and who Angela forgot to tell. She'd never heard of you. So then I looked you up. I did think of going through the Yellow Pages under Escort Services, but a little bird whispered something in my ear, and I phoned directory enquiries and there you were, Lucy Trimble, Private Investigator."

"I haven't been in business long."

"It takes a lot of experience to stay out of trouble, this game. Still, you got on to *me* pretty quick, so I can't brag, can I? There it is, then. Snap," he repeated, and leaned back to show all his teeth.

"What?"

"Snap. Like in the card game. I mean we played the same card. Both of us."

The lanky waiter appeared, a fresh smile on his face. "Everything all right, folks?"

"I'll have another glass of beer," Curnow said.

The waiter looked enquiringly at Lucy. "Some more hot water," she said. "And another tea bag."

"Whatever turns you on."

"Now what?" Lucy asked, when the waiter had gone.

Curnow said, "I'm glad we got that nonsense out of the way. I felt like a schoolboy." He passed a hand over his face. "I never felt right about this job. I usually stick to security jobs. But I've never been offered a job overseas before. It just seemed like a good chance to have a look at Canada. Toronto, anyway. I've messed it up now, though, I suppose. Miss Golden hire you, then?"

"Yes."

"Was I obvious from the start?"

"Oh no, she thought you might be a pervert."

"Me? A pervert? Bloody hell. I'm a widower. I've got a little girl ten years old I'm bringing up myself. Pervert! My little girl dotes on me. What would it be

like for her if ... Bloody hell. What sort of pervert?"
He leaned forward.

Lucy spoke quickly. "I think pervert is too strong.
She meant someone about to pester her."

"Ah." His face grew lighter and the emotion
drained out of it as if a sluicegate had been opened,
leaving him looking exhausted and dull. "That's better. I don't mind that. The other thing is not nice at
all. But even so, look at me. She's much too big for
me. If I were looking, I'd be looking for a small lady.
Smaller than her, anyway. You're more my type." He
tried to smile.

Lucy was sorry to have upset him so much, but at
the same time she realised now that in his present
desire to show he was part of the normal human race,
he was more vulnerable to giving up information than
he might have been. "What *are* you after," she asked.
"Who do you work for?"

"A firm of solicitors in Ilford. They asked me to
find out about Miss Golden, her parents, her background generally, date of birth, place, all that kind of
thing. An identity check."

"Why? Why do they want to know?"

"They didn't tell me. None of my business."

"It's Greta's business. Tell me exactly what they
want to know."

He drew a folded sheet of paper from an inside
pocket. "Greta Golden," he read out, and then the list
of questions about her age, her place of birth, her parents' names, the date of her parents' wedding, and the
dates and places of each of her parents' deaths.

Lucy took the list from him and read it through
again. "Who wants to know?" she asked.

"I told you. I get my orders from a solicitor. I don't know who the end client is."

"Find out," Lucy said.

"But it's none of my business!"

"Why is it secret?"

"It's *private*, not secret. There's a difference."

"Surely Greta has the right to know who is asking about her?"

"But I don't know."

"All right. Now your cover's slipped, it's going to be a lot harder to find the answers to some of these questions about Greta's parents."

"Might be impossible," he conceded.

"I'll tell you the answers. Or Miss Golden will. You tell her who is asking. How about that?"

Curnow considered the offer. "It's not illegal," he said to himself. He looked determinedly at Lucy, and at the list in her hand. "I could spend weeks on this, on my own."

"I could get you the answers by tonight."

"I did want to see Niagara Falls."

She waited to see what he was talking about.

He continued, "You see, I took this job because I've never crossed the pond. All my life I've wanted to see Niagara Falls. If I could get those answers quickly, I could take a day and go down to see the falls tomorrow, instead of sodding about here. Couldn't I? I wouldn't have to tramp round registry offices and chat up people who think I'm a bloody pervert. I could get what I came for and have a day outside, too. Are there coaches to Niagara Falls from here?"

"Lots. Buses, probably every hour or so. Now, what about the other side of the deal?"

"Where's the coach terminus?"

"The bus station is downtown, near here. Where are you staying?"

"Place called The Venture Inn, near Yorkville Village as they call it."

"You are fifteen minutes away, by cab. Now. Your turn."

Curnow took a deep breath. "Listen. First of all, I can't tell you who the ultimate client is, but I can tell you the name of *my* client, the solicitors. Fair enough?"

"I'll see. Go on.

"So, I work for a firm of solicitors called Tucker and Tucker, in Ilford. Now, ask yourself, why would a firm of solicitors in Ilford be enquiring about a woman who lives in Canada?"

Lucy had no problem with this. She even remembered the phrase from novels. "Because they know of something to her advantage?"

"That's it. But they have to be dead sure she is the right one. Now, how would she be connected to — let's say it — the death of someone in England."

"She's in the will."

"Yes, but if she's in the will why don't they get in touch with her?"

Lucy shook her head. "Give up."

"I've thought about this a lot. I think it must be because she's not named, but identified by relationship. If she was a friend, she would be named, like, 'My Friend Greta Golden of such and such an address' and they wouldn't need me to find her. But what you've probably got in the will is just 'and all his issue' or some such, meaning any children of her father's. So they've looked up her father and found he had one daughter. And my job is to find out if your Greta is she. Something like that. When they are sure, someone will get in touch with her." He sat back and picked up his beer. "But in the meantime, they don't want her getting wind of the bequest and sitting on their doorstep."

"And that's all? You just have to make sure Greta is ... Greta?"

"More or less. You understand, all this is conjecture. Just two professional investigators having a chat about the profession."

"I think you're making this all up."

"I told you that I was. But I'm not trying to put you off. That's all I know. Now, what have you got for me?"

"It all sounds a bit fishy. But I'll get all the answers you need from Greta. When shall I meet you tomorrow? What time? Where? I'll see her tonight."

"How long will it take me to get to Niagara Falls and back?"

"It's a day trip. Go down, look at the falls, take a picture, have lunch, come back in the afternoon."

"P'raps I could fly home tomorrow night, if I could get a seat. Let's say I can, then I'll probably be able to meet you for a drink at that hotel, the Royal York, where the airport coach goes from. Give me your phone number. I'll find out about the times of all this now, this afternoon, and phone you."

"It's my assistant's day off, but if I'm not there you can leave a mesage on the machine. I'll pick it up in time."

Curnow drank off the last of his beer. "My daughter will be chuffed at her dad seeing Niagara Falls."

Lucy said, "One thing. You keep saying 'relative.' Couldn't it be something else ... more ... personal? I mean suppose Greta had a former lover who left her everything in his will ... maybe all he remembered was her first name ..."

Curnow shook his head. "I believe you're a romantic, Mrs Trimble. No. I think I answered that. I'll go a bit further. It *is* a relative." He paused. "I suppose I shouldn't have said that, should have left it open. But I told you, I'm not much good at this lark. My specialty's security."

Chapter Seven

Late that afternoon, Lucy was talking to Greta in her apartment on Price Street. The apartment, though constructed to a perfectly conventional plan, had the feeling of an artist's studio at the top of a warehouse, full of light and space uninterrupted by much furniture. The walls, too, seemed oversized because each wall had only one or two small framed photographs in the centre. Greta watched Lucy looking around the room, and grinned. "Welcome to the atelier," she said, confirming Lucy's feeling, if that was what atelier meant. Greta continued, "What you see here is a space furnished by someone who is too big for most spaces, and who hates clambering around a lot of clutter to get to the door, and with walls decorated by a minimalist. Leonard changes the pictures about once a month to give the guests something new to look at. As for me, I think I've got the furniture down to the least I can manage with. Like it?"

"You're practically sitting cross-legged on the floor," Lucy said boldly.

"You've given me an idea. Come back in a month."

"Have you and ... Leonard been together long?"

"Why?"

Lucy blushed. "None of my business. I'm just making conversation."

"Then it must be a *very* significant question. Four years, I think I told you. Now, let's go into the office." She led Lucy into a small room that was the antithesis of the living area, jammed with bookshelves, a divan for overnight guests, and machines — a television set, a computer and printer, a fax and a very complicated-looking telephone. Greta opened a large filing cabinet.

"One: birth certificate," Greta said, sliding it into her fax machine and handing the copy to Lucy.

"You were born in England?"

"I said so, remember. Shale, in Cornwall. There's the date. Two: my mother's birth certificate; Winnipeg, 1929. Three: I don't have my father's birth certificate, but he was English, which may be what this is all about, and they can find that. Four: Here is his 'Legally Landed Immigrant' card. He came over on a ship called the *Canberra,* about two years before he came to Toronto. I seem to remember Ma saying he started off in Edmonton. I don't think he had time to take out citizenship. Five: their wedding certificate, dated, you will notice, seven months before I was born. Looks shocking, doesn't it, but it might have been just premature, as my mother always said. The story that came down to me, told in front of people who might have been around then, is that my mother got tired of being pregnant so she went to England for a rest. There Papa was accidentally drowned by a sudden tidal wave which plucked him off a rock when he

was admiring the sea. The shock of his death induced
a premature labour — me. Six: Here's a picture of the
happy couple on their wedding day in Toronto. And
seven: Here's the same picture in the Cornish paper
that reported the accident. That should satisfy the little man. What is this all about, do you think?"

They were interrupted by the sound of a door
opening and the arrival of Greta's companion, dressed
in black baggy pants, a bomber jacket, a purple T-
shirt and black boots, with a two-day beard. He
looked to Lucy like a street-person who had stolen a
leather coat.

"Hi." He took Lucy's left hand with his right so
that she would not have to turn in her chair. "Leonard
Tacsi." He raised an eyebrow at Greta. "Dinner?"

These two were ten or fifteen years younger than
Lucy, who had come very late to the singles', or
rather, doubles', scene, and she was immediately
intensely curious about them. How did they avoid
getting fraught when their two worlds did not quite
mesh, because she assumed that Tacsi's query meant,
"Where's my dinner?" or "Why is there no goddam
sign of my dinner?" or even, from the look of him,
"Where's my fucking dinner?" and that Greta would
start apologizing and scurrying. But she was wrong.

"No dinner," Greta said.

"No dinner," he repeated, receiving the news
with interest.

"I have to go back to the show. Rejig the booth.
It's a mess."

So "Dinner?" meant simply, "What's the story on
dinner?" without any subtext.

"You be late?" he asked.

"Before you, probably. Right?"

"I'm in a grudge match at the Rivoli. Could be the wee hours."

Greta said to Lucy, "He means he's playing Manitoba Fats at pool." She turned back to Tacsi. "Eat somewhere first and not pizza. It makes you stink of garlic. And don't wake me up when you come in. I have to get up early for the show."

"Likewise. I mean don't wake me in the morning." He leaned over and kissed her. "I'll be out of your way in two minutes. Nice to meet you, Lucy." He disappeared into the bathroom, reappeared to the noise of a flushing toilet, said "Ta-ta," and was gone.

There, thought Lucy. Even allowing for the likelihood that they put on a little Tracy/Hepburn routine in front of strangers, there was no sign of anything fraught about them as they remade their evening. She still had some questions, but there was no need to fill in all the blanks immediately. The point was that no one here was complaining about there being no dinner. After four years, too.

Greta stared at her, waiting.

Lucy remembered what the question was. "Someone wants proof that you are your father's daughter. There's money involved. It's one of the oldest plots in the world. Probably goes like this: Someone's died and left your father some money, money which should now come down to you. But *someone else* has appeared, claiming to be your father, I mean not *your* father, but the man your father was impersonating. Better yet, it is *his* son who has appeared, claiming that *his* father is the true heir, but *he* died thirty years before." Lucy stopped. "Sorry. I'm just playing about. Tell me about your father."

"As far as I know, my father left no relatives or friends behind in England. He was an only child and his parents both died before he left. So my mother told me."

"Perhaps there was a Magwich."

"A what?"

"An old convict your father helped on the marshes come back from Australia with a fortune for his dear boy. Bit late for that, though. You'll have to wait and see." She laughed and waved her hand to signal that her remarks could be ignored.

Greta waited the necessary two seconds to show that she understood that Lucy was not serious, and continued. "In the meantime they want to get these dates straight." She waved the certificates in the air. "This shock-induced labour is all bullshit if you ask me. Just as likely they had to get married, as they used to say."

"What difference would it make?"

"I never knew my father, and my mother cut herself off from her old world when they got married so I never heard any stories about his life before they married, except from her. I've always thought, though, from the picture, that he was a weak man, handsome but soft. Even I wonder if he was my father."

"Do you really?"

"Perhaps my real father took off for the Arctic. Maybe, then, pregnant, she looked around for someone to marry. Aubrey. And let him think he was the real father. You know, seduced him."

"Here we go again. And now your real father has turned up? What's he been doing in England? Anyway, none of this would make any difference to a solicitor, would it? You're still your legitimate father's heir, aren't you?"

Michael Curnow agreed.

He had left a message to confirm that if she would meet him in the York Room at five-thirty, they could have an hour before his bus left for the airport.

He had had a sparkling day, and the pleasure of it showed in the wiry hair that was still slightly tangled. "Coach trip wasn't up to much," he reported. "Not a lot to see. But the falls were smashing. I was glad that the best part of them are in Canada. Listen to me: been here three days and feel like a native. But the Yanks have got the best of everything else, haven't they? On the map it looks like Canada is the bit they didn't want. I went underneath the falls with a party of Japanese, like a lot of little yellow penguins — I mean us, in the raincoats they gave us to walk under the falls with, not the Japs. Afterwards I went on the *Maid of the Mist*, the boat that goes up to the falls. That was something, too. Got soaked." He grinned at the memory and passed a hand over his hair. "Used up two of those instant cameras. Can't wait to show Pamela."

"I'm glad you got what you wanted." Lucy looked pointedly at the clock.

"What? Oh, right." He looked over the papers Lucy had brought, then folded them roughly and stuffed them into his inside pocket. "That should do it. They were nearly all Japanese this afternoon. Did I say that already?"

"Greta said she had grown up with the understanding that her father was an only child and then an orphan before he left England. So if your guess about an inheritance has anything in it, any connection must be a distant one. When will she hear?"

"She might have heard the last of it. Don't forget, you and I have just been speculating. Even if there *is* something, solicitors take their time. They like to seem to earn their money, just like the rest of us."

"Another thing, Greta was born prematurely."

"Yes?" he responded. "Lots were, then. But it just leads to all kinds of speculation, nothing of any import. She's still her father's legal daughter."

"That's what I thought."

"Course, p'raps someone in England knows that Aubrey Golden was congenitally incapable of fathering her, or rather genitally incapable, sorry, no offence, just slipped out." Curnow's face glowed momentarily. "No, that's a lot of nonsense, and might not matter, anyway. Now I'd better be off. I must say you've been a very pleasant factor in my trip. I'm very grateful. If there's anything I can do for you, there's my number." He held out a card.

Lucy took it and looked at her watch. "You've got a few minutes yet. Give me your opinion on something. You do a lot of security work, you say?"

"Mostly, I'd say."

"Investigating shortages from cash registers?"

"Plenty of that. I started out in electronics and rather drifted into rigging up security systems, alarm systems, that sort of thing. But when I went solo it seemed a good thing to call myself by a bigger title in case there was work out there I could do while I waited for the next security job. I don't like it, though, investigating, I mean, and the only reason I took this was because it was a chance to see Niagara Falls."

"But listen to this." And Lucy told him the story of the pharmacist and the cash register, and about the plan that they had worked out to put a video camera over the cash register which he would operate selectively. "Why would he want to do that?" Lucy asked.

Curnow considered. "I don't know. I've never come across that. But I can make a couple of comments. One: I doubt if his tape will stand up as evidence when the defending lawyer finds out that the tape wasn't continuous. How will your employer be able to prove that there's only one thief? Second, I'd be very careful. The man is up to something, so you should strictly follow orders until you figure out what it is. You're being conned."

"That's what I wondered."

"Depend on it; he's up to something. And now I have to go."

"One more minute, please," and in a rush Lucy poured out all the speculations she had already semi-jokingly tried on Greta: the possibility of other claimants appearing, or having appeared, men claiming to be Greta's father who had faked an accidental fall off a cliff, others claiming to be Aubrey Golden's children, even the Magwich story.

Curnow was hugely entertained. "Don't pretend you're not serious," he said. "But I am prepared to look you in the eye and say I know nothing about anyone else in line to the throne. All that happened was someone died, and I was asked to find out what happened to a man named Aubrey Golden after he left

England in 1954, I think it was. I've learned he lived a blameless life in Edmonton for a couple of years, then he came to Toronto and got married. There's no other stone to turn over. I told you you were a romantic." He took her hand, drawing her rather awkwardly to her feet. "And if you're ever in Ilford, very unlikely, look me up, won't you? Meeting you has been the nicest thing about this trip."

Lucy, wedged in too small a space between the coffee table and the chair so that she had to keep her feet in line and twist sideways from the waist, said, "Me and Niagara Falls."

"How about you? If I ever get another case in Toronto, can I look you up?"

Lucy coloured slightly at the appearance of rudeness she was giving by not responding immediately to his invitation with one of her own. "I'd love to see you again. Have a chance to show you the town."

He smiled, apparently satisfied, picked up a small suitcase, looked at her consideringly, significantly, shook his head sadly, and left.

Chapter Eight

"He's satisfied, is he? I'm not. What did he say? I might never hear? Screw that. I want to know." Greta took Lucy's elbow to steer her away from the booth towards a space across the aisle where they could talk without interference from potential buyers.

"There's probably a way. I could ask Jack if you like. Jack Brighton. He's the private detective here in town who found out that Curnow is an investigator. He helped me a lot at the beginning."

"Then let's ask Jack. Can you call him this morning?"

Lucy hesitated. "Yes, but ... this is his work. His job."

"So? That's why we're asking him."

"I've never sort of consulted him before. Just asked him for favours. For myself."

"Got you. This is his living. He might charge a fee. Right. I'll pay anything reasonable."

Brighton said, "This shouldn't be too hard. I have an arrangement with an agency in London. Actually it's just one guy. He'll search the public record. They keep everything in one place over there. Somersetshire House, it's called. They can tell right away who died lately, see if a will has been probated. Something like that. But it *is* his bread, Lucy," he added, confirming Lucy's newly arrived instinct. "Who's your client? She know you are asking me for help?"

"Her name is Greta Golden, and I told her about you."

"How much is she good for?"

"Don't go over the top."

"Two hours work for my English contact — say two hundred bucks — a hundred for me, plus phone, faxes, so maybe four hundred altogether, plus there's you."

"Seems high."

"It's what my podiatrician charges to fix an ingrown toenail if he has to use anaesthetic."

"Go ahead. Send me a breakdown with your bill. She'll understand. She's in business herself."

"It's four o'clock there now. I'll fax this so he can put someone to work on it first thing in the morning. He has a couple of what he calls his colleagues — they're two old ladies who work for him sometimes to help out their pensions — I think they used to work in legal offices. We could hear back by noon tomorrow."

"This is exciting," Greta said. "Do you need an assistant if I ever get bored with native crafts?"

While she waited for Jack to report back, Lucy arranged with a security company to install the video camera after the pharmacy was closed. She made one more puzzled enquiry of Coopman, but the pharmacist stuck to his story that the reason he wanted to stop and start the tape was to save money.

Lucy put the phone down and called down the corridor to Peter Tse, who was working in his office. "Would you like some coffee?"

He appeared in the doorway. "Problem?"

"Sort of. A puzzle. Did you hear me on the phone?"

"No, but usually when you offer to go get the coffee it's because you want to talk about somethink."

"Am I that bad? I'll try and remember to just offer you some coffee one of these days, just for the love of you."

"Leave your door open. I'll 'ear you come back."

When she returned from the Portuguese café on the corner, he had locked his door and was sitting waiting in her office. "Bloke came in covered in blood, talking about some bird he wanted you to find. A falcon. I told him you were too busy to go bird 'unting."

"You did right. I am. I've got a genuine mystery on my hands." She brought him up to date on the story of the pharmacist's cash register.

"'E's up to something, Lucy," Tse said, sagely.

"I know that. What?"

"You'll 'ave to wait and see when you run the tape, won't you? I mean see what 'e decides to get pictures of. Will 'e know how to run it 'imself?"

"I don't think so."

"Don't show him. Wait until you've seen what 'e's got pictures of."

It was an obvious answer, and one that allowed her to forget about Coopman temporarily.

"In the meantime," Tse said, "I've thought some more about the other thing. The two tearaways 'oo pinched the car, found the body, got stopped by the police? You said it was too coincidental, or rather, that's what you *thought*. Right? That's because I was wrong about the car. See, they didn't steal it — it belonged to one of them. They just found the body when they opened the trunk to load in a TV set one of them 'ad found the night before. So now they 'ad to find out 'oo 'e was, and 'oo put him there."

"Why? Obviously someone put the body there because it was the first hiding place they could find. Nothing to do with your two, just the kind of neighbourhood they park in. So all they have to do is drive back to the spit and throw the body in the lake."

"Yeah? I'll get back to you."

Brighton said, "There are three possibilities. I'm reading off the fax now. A lot of people called Golden died in the last six months — you notice how I'm avoiding calling them the Golden people? — but these three are from London, and all of them left significant sums of money, enough worth suing for. And, narrowing it down still further, there is one man, Geoffrey Golden, who was worth four hundred and fifty thousand pounds — say a million bucks, whose estate is being handled by a legal firm in, wait for it, Ilford, solicitors called Wylie and Wylie. So that's your man. Do you want anything else from my English investigator? So far his bill is only seventy-five pounds. Probably paying one of his old ladies ten pounds for an hour's research, but that's not our business, and seventy-five pounds is about the minimum."

"What was the name of those solicitors?"

"Wylie and Wylie."

Greta said, "I'd better have my lawyer do this."

The next day, Greta called Lucy. "The miracle of the fax," she said. "A couple of years ago we would have been writing back and forth for weeks. Wylie and Wylie said they had started a search for me — wasn't that what your detective pal was doing — ?"

"Yes, but he was working for someone else, one of the other heirs, or all of them."

"Do you have any names?"

"He was hired by another firm of lawyers called Tucker and Tucker."

"I'll get my lawyer to ask Wylie what's up with Tucker, shall I? But listen to the rest of their message, 'All his money is left to his brothers and sister, or their heirs, in equal portions.' They don't say how many, though."

They had to wait another day.

"Here it is," Greta said. "I'm quoting: Geoffrey Golden had three brothers and two sisters. Two brothers and the sisters have been informed by the solicitor. The third brother, Aubrey, left England for Canada forty-five years ago. A search has revealed that he died in an accident in Cornwall thirty-nine years ago, leaving a wife and an infant daughter, Greta. The wife and daughter returned to Canada, where Greta Golden is now living in Toronto. Under the terms of the will she will inherit more than a hundred thousand pounds. Evidence of the marriage has been documented, as has the death of Aubrey Golden, and the birth of the daughter, Greta. The solicitors will be contacting Greta in due time."

Greta finished reading. "That should do it," she said.

Two weeks later Greta called Lucy and told her that she had been asked to send the name of her solicitor so that the estate could be settled. This she had done, and now she waited for her money. "How much do I owe you, by the way? We've paid off all your helpers, haven't we?"

"There's just me left. I think four hundred would be fair."

"Make it five. I'm rich."

"I have to go to New York for a couple of days," Johnny said.

Lucy's heart lifted at the prospect of a few days on her own; they had lived together long enough for that. But the lift was accompanied by a slight pang, because she had never been to New York herself. "Want me to come?" she asked. "What do you have to do?"

"Look at a couple of two-year-olds Jesse Feeld's

been offered."

Jesse Feeld was a baseball player who owned some racehorses.

"Then I'd just be in the way."

"You'd be on your own a lot," he agreed.

"I'll stay here, then. When will you be back?"

"I've booked a flight to come back on Sunday morning. Do whatever you want."

Lucy couldn't tell if he was hoping she would stay home, or was indifferent, or just feeling slightly miffed because she so easily chose not to insist on going with him. So, in a tiny way, the situation was once more fraught. But he must be aware that she was finding herself steadily less interested in these horse racing outings than she had been a year ago, when she first met him. The brilliant green turf, the magnificently polished horses, and the bright splashes of the jockeys' colours — they were all fading into familiarity. The root of an interest in horse racing is betting, finding winners, and since Lucy had almost no taste for the gambling, she had begun to take a book to read at the track, which irritated Comstock, for whom horse racing was his whole life.

But this wasn't actual racing, just looking at the animals. "I'll stay here," she repeated. "Which hotel will you be staying at?"

"The Alexander. On 72nd street. Why?"

"So I can call you if I get lonely."

"I thought you seemed sort of busy."

Too busy for him, did he mean? Lucy searched for some space among the eggshells. "I've got my crocheting," she said, trying to brush away their touchiness with a bright smile.

And then, on Wednesday evening, when he had gone, she decided that she had reacted poorly, that she ought to have been more eager, and she booked a seat on a plane for the next morning.

Before she left she called the Alexander Hotel to warn Johnny she was coming, that she would wait for him to come back to the hotel after he had finished looking at horses. She asked Peter Tse to keep an eye on her office, and answer her phone if he felt like it.

"Pleasure," she said in answer to the U.S. immigration officer's question. She wondered, since the Immigration Department had set up their gate at Toronto's Pearson Airport, if they would be legally entitled to take someone who had gone through the barrier into American custody. Was the soil on the other side of the barrier temporarily American?

The officer, a boy with a putty face and thick colourless hair, leaned back, leafing slowly through her passport. "What do you do, ma'am?"

"I'm a private investigator."

He looked up so sharply that a hank of hair fell over one eye. He lifted the hair clear and took a good look at her, then grinned. "Ah, shit," he said to himself, softly, then, to Lucy, "That right?"

"That's right."

"Well, holy cow," he said, then turned to the man in the next booth. "Got the winner, today, Lou," he said. "Private eye, in drag. Beats your contortionist this morning all to hell, don' it?"

"Hell, no," Lou said. "Private eyes in drag are a dime a dozen. Contortionists are *rare*. We'll have to get a decision. Fred!" he called to a third oficer. "Which is worth more? ..."

"What are you talking about?" Lucy demanded to know. What were they judging? Freaks?

The official showed her the passport. It was Johnny's. But the explanation was obvious, and she had made their day, so her birth certificate got her through the gate. Johnny, of course, must have simply left his passport behind, after he had dug it out of the drawer. Unless he hadn't gone to New York at all? No, the Alexander had him booked in. Right?

At La Guardia she accepted the cab offered, a car with no shock absorbers driven by a mute Haitian. The ride into town, especially along Franklin Roosevelt Drive, reminded Lucy of films she had seen of a winter sport where four men hurtled down a snowy ramp on a piece of wood.

There was a problem at the hotel desk. Johnny was staying in a double room, but he had not, of course, prepared the hotel for the possible arrival of Lucy. The desk clerk, a jowly young man who looked to Lucy as if he had heard it all and never believed any of it, said, "Listen, lady, I can't let anyone into that room who isn't booked in, which means just one guy gets in. He could have informed us of your arrival but he didn't. So ..." he turned his palms upwards and looked away.

Lucy said, "I'll try again in a couple of hours, then. Where can I leave my bag?"

"Wassat, lady?"

"My bag. Where can I leave it?"

"You mean you want to leave it here somewhere?"

"Yes. So I can go for a walk."

"When are you coming back?" This, his tone suggested, was kind of pushy, wanting to leave your bag, in a hotel.

Then someone behind her picked up the bag and took her elbow. It was the elevator operator. "I'll look after it," he said.

They walked across the lobby so that he could show her the cubbyhole he kept bags in. "You won't need a claim check," he said. "I'll know you."

"Why is the man at the desk like that?" she asked.

"Because he's an asshole," he said, in the same tone as he might have said 'because he's from Arizona,' identifying the type and its characteristics, not judging it.

She walked out to Columbus Avenue and turned north, uptown. She guessed that if she returned about six, Johnny would have ended his working day and might have come back to his room before going out for the night. She walked up to 92nd street, window shopping, and turned back when the shops seemed to end. At 72nd street again, she ate a toasted bagel in a coffee shop and crossed to Amsterdam Avenue. By three o'clock she had done both sides of Amsterdam for about twenty blocks, and she moved over to Broadway. The whole town seemed like a toyshop, windows crammed with things Toronto had no room for, specialty shops that required a huge population with kaleidoscopic tastes to make them viable. One store sold only yoga supplies — books, mats, videos; another was devoted to paperweights.

It was something to look at to fill in the time until Johnny returned.

At six she walked back to the hotel but Johnny still hadn't arrived and she collected her bag from the elevator man and sat in the lobby until eight. Now she began to feel concerned. The same clerk was still on the desk, and she asked him if he would have a room, later, if Johnny stayed out too late for her to wait.

"You want to book a room now?" he asked.

She explained her predicament again.

"You want a room *now*?"

"No. Perhaps later."

"I can't keep it on hold, lady. I've got a couple of rooms, but they could go anytime."

"I'd better book one *now*, then."

She left her bag in her room and walked out on to Columbus to find dinner, settling for an Italian restaurant where she was served an enormous plate of spaghetti, for which, she discovered, she had almost no appetite. She left the restaurant and walked back to 72nd street and her hotel. Johnny still had not returned, and she began to feel genuinely forlorn.

As she explained to Nina later, "Here I was in New York for the first time in my life, but I felt as if I was on hold, or New York was. You've had that experience, surely, of not being able to settle to anything because you're waiting for someone to turn up, so instead of experiencing it and enjoying it you are just putting in time, waiting. Add to that the fact that the only person I'd spoken to was that pig of a desk clerk — except for the elevator operator — and you have my first trip to New York."

"Did he turn up that night?"

"No, he didn't, and I don't know if this has happened to you, but now I was seriously fed up with him. It was his fault, even if he was dead."

"He didn't expect you, though."

"Never mind. He should have been there. My big larky outing was turning to ..."

"Ratshit?"

"That's it. So when he did turn up, it took me a long time to make myself agreeable."

"When did he appear?"

"The next afternoon. Friday afternoon."

"What did you do with yourself on Friday?"

"Exactly. What did I do with myself? I decided not to come back every two hours but leave a message to say I would be back for dinner and do the town. It didn't work, though, because while I was getting up a head of steam, wondering why he didn't appear, I was also, slightly, wondering if he was lying mugged somewhere. I'll be careful about surprises, in future."

"I would if I were you," Nina said. "What did you do?"

"Walked across Central Park then down Fifth Avenue, and across to Times Square. It was a lovely day, and I should have had a marvellous outing, but all the time I was looking at my watch. Finally I went back to the hotel around four o'clock, wondering if I should come home right then, but he was waiting for me at the hotel. So then it was all right."

"Was it?"

"No. Well, more or less. He explained that he'd been out on Long Island the evening I arrived and some trainer had offered him a bed for the night so he stayed out there."

"Did you do the town, then? Where did you go?"

"Oh, Greenwich Village, and Soho, and the South Seaport, and the street markets on Canal Street. All my suggestions, all the places I'd heard about, mainly from you. I wish *you'd* been there."

"Did you see a play?"

"Yes, but I don't remember the name of it. In the end I just felt, I don't know, stupid, because I didn't have a very good time, and so he didn't, either."

At this point she felt shy of telling Nina the whole story.

She had moved into his room where he loved her agreeably but not very vigorously, but he seemed very busy; there were messages waiting whenever they returned to the hotel, and the phone rang often when they were there. Seven or eight times she answered it when she was alone in the room, only to have the caller hang up when she spoke. She joked about it to Johnny, wondering what kind of people he associated with in New York, and it was not until Sunday morning when they were on the plane back that she realized what was happening. Welcome to the real world, she told herself, feeling a return of the naivete she thought she had left behind in Longborough, Ontario.

Chapter Nine

Greta's voice began as soon as Lucy picked up the phone. "There's been a challenge," she said. "The others claim that the dead brother did not know that Aubrey had married before he died, and the intent of his will was to reward the remaining brothers and sisters, the ones he thought had survived. They also claim I'm not my father's daughter, that my mother married Aubrey Golden just to give me a name. It's possible. I *was* a seven-month baby."

"We talked about all that, Michael Curnow and I, and it doesn't make any difference."

"They say there is an intent to defraud, and the courts could agree."

"But even if it's true, your mother couldn't have been intending to defraud them forty years down the road!"

"My lawyer says it's an interesting question. One that needs lawyers to sort it out, he means. But setting aside the question of a juicy legal bonanza, he agrees. Their claim is absurd, but you can't stop them making it. You can see now what happens in those family squabbles that always sound like horror shows from the outside. Two brothers or two sisters fighting over a legacy and getting very quickly to the point where the fight is what matters, hating each other, spending the whole legacy on lawyers just to win. My lawyer had a friendly little chat with the English lawyer, off the record, totally illegal, I suspect, and what it seems to have come down to is that my father waved his family goodbye forty-five years ago, came here, and told everyone including my mother that his parents were dead. They weren't; they were destitute, though, and in bad health, and one reason my father left was to avoid having to help look after them. He told everyone here, including my mother, that he was an only child. Figure that out. He simply cut himself off ..."

"Were the brothers and sisters all poor, too?"

"I would think. They don't have any money now, anyway. Two of them are on what they call 'income supplement' — welfare?"

"Why wouldn't they just split the legacy? They'd be quite well off, wouldn't they?"

"Now you're being sensible and logical. That's what I said, and, of course, that's what my lawyer asked, without my prodding. The fact is, they hated my father because he ran off, leaving them with the problem of their parents. And apparently, without my father's wages they were that much worse off — I don't know. It all sounds to me as if daddy, as I never learned to call him, was something of a bastard. And that's what's animating them now. The money is not so important as getting their revenge by trying to do me out of my father's share of the will."

"How did the brother who died — where did he get his money?"

"Apparently he was a used-car dealer in a place called Manor Park, which is near Ilford. Retired, but that was how he made his fortune."

"There's more money in used cars than I would have thought," Lucy said. "So what now?"

My lawyers have started an investigation."

"Into what?"

"They hardly know. They want proof I'm their niece, for one thing. How will they get that?"

"I've no idea. I'll have to think about it."

"Will you?"

"What?"

"Think about it. Take me on. Prove that I'm Aubrey Golden's daughter?"

Lucy said, "Suppose there's something in it?"

"Supposing I'm not? Then find out whose daughter I am. It's not the will. This money won't make any difference to me. My mother left a lot of insurance, and the business is doing well. But I'm fascinated. Maybe I really was sired by a young politician on his way up, some womanizer now in high office. Could have ruined his career back then, but nowadays it would help him get elected. I fancy a brilliant Québecois lawyer giving Ma a tumble in Martinique, say, when she was on a buying trip. Something like that would account for my remarkable intelligence."

Maybe we just have to find a tall senator, Lucy thought. She said, "Let's not let this run away from us. This is one of those things like a self-fulfilling prophecy. These bitter relatives of yours have manufactured a grudge — well, no — your father does sound like a case — they've allowed a grudge to come between them and their common sense, and you are doing the same. And because they are objecting, you are doing a 'where there's smoke there might be fire' number."

Greta spoke into her thoughts. "Maybe he was a priest. Be a bishop by now, wouldn't he? Find him. Find a tall bishop."

"You want me to establish that in all probability your father was who you think he was, given the suddenly discovered aunts and uncles, and if he wasn't, who is? Based on something that might have happened forty years ago?"

"That's it. Yes."

"I need to think."

"Before you say yes? Why? I'll pay you for it."

"I need to think about where to begin, how long it might take, and how much it might cost you, for starters."

"Never mind all that. If you can see where to begin, will you?"

"I'll call you tomorrow."

"Say yes, though, won't you? It's not the will, Lucy, and it's not even the possibility I might be a kind of royal bastard. I'd like to know, is all. Look, how far back do you yourself go? How many generations?"

"On my father's side we were Loyalists who crossed the border after the American Revolution. On my mother's side there was a Welsh shepherd who came over before Confederation."

"Dear Jesus, how Canadian can you get? Practically aboriginal. Look at me. I don't know anything beyond my mother. She was an only child, and she died not speaking to *her* mother. I was always taught that my father was the end of *his* line, too. I'd like some ancestors. Why did my father say he was the only child? *Was* he my father? Find out, would you?"

"All right. One thing's clear now. Remember, that private detective, Michael Curnow, wasn't working for Wylie and Wylie who are handling the will, but for another firm, Tucker and Tucker. I think they must have been hired by the relatives, and they hired Curnow."

"Does it make any difference?"

"Only that Curnow probably went back and told them they were wasting their time. He was here to find the evidence to disprove your claim, but he found the opposite. Not that he cared."

Lucy put down the phone, thinking that there must be money in native crafts, too. She called Jack Brighton and arranged to meet him in his office.

A major distraction was exactly what she needed while she found out what she felt about Johnny. She had no claim on him, but she had thought they were living, had been living for some months, in unspoken commitment to each other. Now a small crack had appeared in the solid ice they had been skating on. What she wanted was time to wait and see how she felt when she woke up in the morning. No confrontations, no recriminations, no arguments, no fights, and no reconciliations. Just to know would be enough.

First she had to look at the video cassettes she had retrieved from the pharmacy.

Peter Tse kept a television set and a VCR in his office to amuse himself on dull afternoons, and they looked at the cassettes together. There were only two. Peter said, "I fink you're being conned, Lucy."

"Why?"

"It's phony. I don't fink he wants a tape of people stealing at all."

"What does he want, then?"

"You saw the tape. What's 'e got a picture of? A lovely pair of bristols from an unusual perspective, that's what 'e's got. And that maybe is what 'e wanted."

"Lovely pair of what? Oh, you mean the dark-haired girl. He's spending a lot of money to get that."

Tse grinned. "They do, them guys. Obsessed, is what they are. Obsessed."

"Don't be silly. I can't believe that even if he's dement-ed by the sight of a pair of ... what was that word?"

"Bristols."

"Where does it come from? What's a bristol? I mean a real bristol."

"Don't ask me. I brought the word over on the boat."

"My instincts tell me you are half right. I do think he's up to something, but not just taking pictures of his staff."

"Did they have any perverts in that library where you worked?"

"The place was full of them. Now let me write my report. He'll be here in an hour."

A knock on the door preceded the head that looked quizzically around it to see if it was all right to come in. Lucy nodded, and her client crossed the room and sat down opposite her.

Lucy came to the point quickly.

"Mr. Coopman," she said. "The tapes don't show any of the the three women dipping into the till."

"So what do you deduce from that, Mrs. Sherlock?" Coopman asked.

Irritated, because she had long been tired of clients who did not take her seriously enough, even though they hired her, she said, "The name is Trimble. There are several possibilities. One is that you aren't activating the tape enough. A second is that they know about it so they are lying low until you give up on the camera."

"Any others?"

"That's really for you to think about, Mr. Coopman. You paid me to investigate and make a report. If you want a recommendation, then I suggest you run the tape continuously. That's my report. Here." She handed him the draft she had just printed.

He put the report down without looking at it. "You've done what you were paid for," he said agreeably.

Lucy had been expecting some irritation or dismay at the paucity of her findings. Coopman, though, seemed content. Perhaps Peter was right. "You don't want me to run a continuous tape?" she asked.

"I might," he said. He didn't move. "I'll let you know."

Now he winked at her. "Given you something to think about, I'll bet. Eh?"

"As long as you're satisfied," she said, wondering now, though not very deeply, what sort of little game Coopman was playing.

"Any other suggestions?"

Lucy said, "None. Except that someone may be getting to that money when it's out of camera range."

Coopman jerked his head up in a show of surprise and let out two or three barks of laughter. "Hey!" he said. "Hey. Let me think about that. I think you're wrong but you've earned your fee."

"You sure you don't want me to make a continuous tape?"

"Oh, no." The look on his face suggested that Lucy should guess again. Now she began to wonder if the whole thing were not a contrivance, some elaborate game in which the surveillance camera played a part though not the one it was hired for. She was sorry she had not looked more carefully at the tape, because now she was sure that it wasn't a thief he was watching for, but something else, yet his present lack of any furtiveness or embarrassment probably ruled out Peter's suggestion. Perhaps he was simply enamoured of one of the girls, all of her, and jealousy made him want to catch her being nice to a boyfriend. Lucy gave up.

"I've found out what I wanted to know," he said.

"You found out that the staff are honest."

"That, too," he said, mysteriously.

And then Lucy had spent enough time on a problem that no longer interested her. She stood up. "There's a per diem rental for the camera. Shall I call the agency and have them take it out after the store is closed?"

"Oh, yes. Won't need it any more, will we?" Coopman sounded sad and weary. Lucy realized that he didn't want to leave, because the next move was his. As long as he was talking to her he was postponing his worries. She held out her hand. "Sorry I couldn't catch the thief," she said.

"No, you're not, are you?"

"Not really. I'm just glad it wasn't one of the girls."

He stood up reluctantly, then paused. "Not at the cash register, anyway," he said. "But you did your job." He took out his wallet and counted out some bills. "Here."

"I'll make you out a receipt." She turned to her computer.

"Don't bother. This is something I won't be declaring."

"I don't have a clue," Brighton said. "But I can tell you who to ask." He gave Lucy the name of a well-known journalist who was also the theatre reviewer for a radio station. John Board had begun life as a lawyer, and now, in his spare time, he wrote two books a year on aspects of the law that the public might be interested in. "He just wrote a book on DNA. He'd know. What about this other thing: 'Creating an heir with intent to defraud.' Sounds like fun."

"My client's solicitors are responding to that."

"I'll bet they are. Who's paying?"

"My client."

"And the bill for contesting the will?"

"How would I know?"

"I'll tell you. It comes out of the estate. Maybe those English lawyers should be sued for having a financial interest in the pursuit of bullshit claims against the estate. But they never are, those guys. Anyway, my bill is fifty."

"You serious?"

"Sure I am. I thought we were into a new under-standing. I'm being consulted. Include my fee with the next bill to your client."

"You *are* serious, aren't you? You are going to charge me every time I speak to you."

"Just every time you've got a client. Gossip is still free. Listen, fifty is *cheap*. If I were a urologist with my own clinic ..."

"A what?"

"Never mind. I was talking to my father last night. He's saving up to have his prostate repaired."

"In future, then, I won't ask you. I'll consult you."

"That's the idea. We can still have a little chat from time to time, but not if you are on a retainer."

It was embarrasssing, but only in the way all such ini-tiations into the real world are. From the time she had been given Jack's name when she had needed help to set up shop as an investigator, she had turned to him repeatedly, and he had always been available. But now, he was saying, she was a big girl, grown up, on her own, and it was time she observed the rules of the big people. Thank God she had felt it coming and warned Greta — who had needed no warning — that there would be a fee. From now on she would be con-scious of those rules whenever money was involved.

How long had Jack been waiting for her to offer to pay for advice? She ran their history back through her mind and was comforted to know that it wasn't all that long. In the beginning she had done a couple of jobs for him, for which she had been paid. One of them turned into her first big success. Then, too, she had faithfully turned out to laugh whenever he did a stint as a stand-up comedian, about once a month. So far, then, surely, she had not been freeloading that much. But now Jack had formally declared that he was a professional, and so was she. Lucy pondered the rest of the relationships she had formed since she arrived in Toronto, wondering who else might be waiting for her to join the adult world where you paid for services if they were rendered by people who made their living that way. It was a bit like learning that you have not been taught proper table manners.

She began with her landlord, Peter Tse, who had looked after her when she first arrived to take over her cousin's office. Was it time for her to show her appreciation beyond paying her rent regularly? Probably. But how? She couldn't for the life of her figure out what you did for a middle-aged Chinese cockney who had once, only semi-jokingly, told her he had a "pisspot full of money." Perhaps just for now, find out his birthday and take him out to lunch that day? Something like that. And buy a new client chair so that she could give Peter back the one he had loaned her a year ago?

Then there was Nina, Nina Sobczyk, the travel agent in the office across Queen Street who had first raised the alarm when she had seen Lucy's cousin lying on the floor of the office. Nina had since become a friend, a confidant, and very much the city mouse to Lucy's country mouse — even, out of her more sophisticated background, solving one of Lucy's cases for her. Now Lucy became uncomfortable, because that spring Nina had taken Lucy to Montreal for a nearly free weekend put together out of a travel agent's perks.

Even the fare was half-price. At the time Lucy had
assumed that Nina had a drawer full of freebies, but
now she saw that the freebies, which were probably
not unlimited, and on which she probably had a lot of
calls, came because of the business Nina generated,
and therefore it was at least time for Lucy to persuade
everyone she knew to book their travel through Nina.

There didn't seem to be anyone else who was waiting for her to grow up. Her cousin's lawyer had been
very helpful, but she'd paid his bill, so she was surely
not beholden to him. She realized, with some gratitude
now, that she must have presented a figure of helpless-
ness to all these people when she first arrived, a middle-aged child. But now she had come of age, emerged
into the jungle with no family mentors to guide her.
Hers was an extreme case, but some element of it must
be present whenever a woman becomes newly independent and has to learn all the codes the world has
developed for knowing when something is being
offered for free, and when payment is expected. Once,
Lucy thought only widows felt like this, but there are
a lot more of us around now.

Chapter Ten

"I know hardly anything about those days. My mother never reminisced; she seemed to have left that world behind. I grew up sleeping under the counter, if you know what I mean. All my mother's energy was poured into the business, and all her friends were connected with it, including, I think, her lovers. She was old-fashioned enough to keep me and her lovers apart, but when I grew old enough to wonder, I realized they did exist, and then later I pieced together two significant affairs, one out of all her trips to Boston, and the other in England which must have been a sort of long weekend tacked on to the end of every business trip. I don't know who they were, but I know they existed because occasionally she would own to a special knowledge of England or Boston such as only an insider would have. And once or twice she would say, 'Someone I know in England told me ...' or, 'A person I know in Boston says ...' followed by a bit of information like, 'You should never go to the Chichester Festival while the races are on,' or 'Afternoon tea at the copley-plaza in Boston is as

good as Brown's in London.' See? Some real afficiona-
do, and never a man or a woman, always 'someone' or
'a person' so certainly a man, but someone she didn't
want to talk about. But these don't matter. You need
people from 1958. Now, who is there?"

At Greta's suggestion, they were drinking coffee in
Danieli's, a restaurant near her warehouse. "Come to
the office," Greta had said, "And we'll go out. We'll
keep getting interrupted in my office."

"First, no great-aunts or uncles. Right?"

"Not on my father's side, as you know. My mother was born and grew up in Winnipeg, then, after college, like all good Manitobans, she came to Toronto."

"Where do they go to die? Good Manitobans."

"Victoria, if they grew up on the prairies. But I
know my grandfather died quite young, in his fifties.
He worked for the railroad, I think, but I don't know
which one. My mother quarrelled with my grand-
mother and never made it up."

"You don't know what about?"

"Something stupid like Granny finding Ma's
diaphram, I would think." Greta shook her head.
"Granny was a strict Mennonite. Are they against
birth control? Look, this family stuff is embarrassing.
Fact is, my mother hated her mother and wanted
nothing to do with her and wouldn't even talk about
her, except to tell me she was dead. 'I wiped her out
of my life,' was all she would say. She sounds kind of
terrible, doesn't she, my old ma, and I know she could
be ruthless. Tough, anyway. Maybe she had to be to
make it on her own. But she was a good mother. I
don't feel nearly as screwed-up as most of my friends
with doting parents are. They're all in analysis.

"For a start, then, the people you might track down are my mother's Toronto friends from those days."

"When did she graduate from Manitoba?"

"1957."

"Do you have a class picture, something like that?"

She shook her head. "The more you ask, the more I realize how careful my mother was to seal up her past. I have no pictures, letters, invitations to proms, none of that stuff. It's as if she torched the lot."

"You sure she graduated in '57?"

"Yes. Yes, I think so. That date stuck in my head early."

"Do you have *any* pictures from that time?"

"None."

"I told you this might be expensive."

"I don't care. There's a lovely deep dark secret somewhere, and it is time I knew. I still think my father screwed Ma the night before he became prime minister." She put down her empty cup and picked up her purse. "But you need money. Here. Here's five hundred out of petty cash. Do you have any credit cards?"

"Two. A personal one, and one for the agency."

"Perfect. While you're working for me you won't be working for anyone else, will you?"

"Not actively. I've got a couple of other irons in the fire."

"Really? That's not just bullshit to impress the customers?" Greta laughed. "Never mind. What's the limit on your card?"

"Five thousand."

"Where will you start?"

"The class of '57?"

"If there are any roots, that's where they will be. There is one person, though, you might want to talk to right here. He wasn't part of the Manitoba group, and I don't think he was around them much in that year, though I suppose he might have met them. At any rate, he wasn't my mother's friend, even though he was there all the time I was growing up. Actually he is still around but I never see him. His name is Jim McSweeney, and he lives on Ward's Island, and when I was a child he took an interest in me, like a substitute uncle. Used to buy me books — all my good books came from him — and sometimes he took me and Ma out for a treat. We saw the first *101 Dalmatians* with him, and he took us to the pantomime once or twice — you remember Eric Christmas? No, I guess not. Anyway, Uncle Jim, as I learned to call him, might have some suggestions. And now that we've mentioned *him*, I'm going to look him up, myself. What a lot of memories this is churning up. But he is a nice man. Go see him yourself."

"What does he do?"

"He's a freelance editor and reader for publishers. He's lived on the island for about twenty years."

In the year she had lived in Toronto, Lucy had never made the trip to Ward's Island, perhaps a half a mile away across Lake Ontario. "Make sure to take the right ferry," Greta warned her. "Not the big one that goes to Centre Island. The Ward's Island ferry is the small one that takes trucks and residents of the island over." She explained, "There's a community there, a few hundred houses, that has kind of evolved from an older community of summer homes, built before the days of universal air-conditioning by people who could afford to get away from the humidity of Toronto in the summer."

"Is there a beach there?"

"There's a beach, yes, but you'll freeze your tits off if you try to swim in Lake Ontario." She shuddered. "I've visited the place a few times; I know one or two people there, but I can't see the attraction — in winter I think the last ferry goes over at ten! — though it must be there, because they go on and on about the quality of their life. The rednecks on council and up at Queen's Park keep trying to expropriate them to make another park, but they aren't doing any harm and we don't need another park there, so leave them alone, I say."

"How do I get to the ferry?"

"Take the subway to Union, then there's a little street railway that runs along the harbour front. The first stop is the ferry dock."

Lucy was surprised by the difference between the islanders she had imagined from Greta's description and those on the ferry. As Greta had described them, she had thought there would be fifty or sixty people on the ferry all hugging each other with relief and affection now they were once more on the way to their island Arcadia after a foray across the asphalt of the Toronto jungle. She expected a lot of hair, loose cotton garments made in Malaysia, and that, close up, the women, and some of the men, would smell of tarragon.

In fact, the crowd on the ferry could have passed any Saturday afternoon on Queen Street. There were perhaps one or two more real sandals from the Third

World, as opposed to the German up-market kind favoured by Queen Street, and the rest of the clothes were utilitarian, rather than fashionable in any sense, not worn as costumes, but the sort of clothes that had emerged as the most useful for a day that would include cycling to the ferry (because there were more cyclists than in an average Toronto crowd, especially among the old men), shopping in the Eaton Centre, and going to the cinema: khaki mostly, with back-packs. And though she counted six people who greet-ed each other, most of them didn't. More people said hello when she was shopping at Queen and Egerton, Lucy thought. It was about like the crowd on the late night Greyhound bus from Toronto to Longborough. She tried to think of a situation in which all these peo-ple would look at home, what they looked as if they had in common, and came to the conclusion that although any one of them might be a collector door-to-door for an ecological group (most of them looked slightly underpressed), they were otherwise as a group heterogeneous enough to make a pollster's day.

And yet, with her back to the skyline, watching the island approach, she did feel that she was joining a small community, and now the people on the ferry just looked like the summer residents of one of the cottage areas near Longborough — Rice Lake, perhaps — dressing down to look like the permanent residents.

She had called ahead and been given instructions for the seven minute walk to McSweeney's house: down the main street, across the bridge over the lagoon, and back along a smaller street to Quail Street. McSweeney was waiting for her at the end of his garden, a telescope in hand, scanning the road for signs of life. When she was about twenty yards away, he focussed on her with a sharp twist of his wrist, shouted "Ahoy, there," opened the gate, and added, "Come aboard."

He was a tall, white-haired, mostly bald, red-faced man dressed in the ragged remains of a pair of white duck trousers and a khaki shirt, and wearing clogs. Lucy edged around him to walk up the path, then waited for him to precede her into the house, which he did, leading her finally to the most dilapidated armchair she had ever seen, in a room so heavily encrusted with the details of McSweeney's life that at first, to Lucy's eye — still the eye of a Kingston, Ontario housewife — it seemed filthy, the dwelling of a tramp. And in spite of the greeting, there was nothing at all nautical about it.

Then the number of books, papers, and manuscripts lying about led her to see that McSweeney was at least an erudite tramp, and her eyes focussed properly like someone understanding how to look at a new kind of art and she saw that the room was much more clean than dirty; what looked like rubbish at a glance was, seen object by object, the material of an original way of life — a bowl, two vases — one full of wild flowers — a stapler, a pair of running shoes, a pile of clean, unsorted laundry, a basket of dirty unsorted laundry, three mugs, a large wooden bowl full of writing implements — pens, pencils and marking crayons — a tea-tray filled with boxes of paperclips, thumtacks, a roll of postage stamps, envelopes, postcards, five toy soldiers, three small brass tins labelled "Maggots," "Worms," and "Bait," a large alarm clock showing the correct time. All this on a table about fifteen feet long and six feet wide, around which were placed seven or eight kinds of seats — two kitchen chairs (one backless), a milking stool, a metal trunk with a cushion, a "Director's" chair, a fake Jacobean oak throne, and a small wooden hall bench.

"I know where *everything* is," McSweeney said, emphasizing "everything" in imitation of a proud child.

"On the table," Lucy said.

"Well done. But that's my line, of course, if you ask me first, but I could see you weren't going to. Now turn round."

"Turn *round*?" Was he going to assault her, playfully, of course, from behind? Goose her?

"Yes. Sit in that chair with your back to the table."

Lucy did as she was told, fearful that the chair was rigged to tip her through a trapdoor into a root cellar full of McSweeney's old clothes.

"Now, how many things can you remember on the table? Here's a pen. Here's a piece of paper. And here's something to write on. Now. Go! While I get lunch."

"You want me to write down all I can remember?"

"That's it. Go!"

"Why?"

"It's the only form of entertainment I can offer you while I get lunch. Otherwise I shall be forced to shout pleasantries through the door. Now, Go!"

Lucy did as she was told and had reached sixteen when McSweeney returned with two plates, which he put on the table, clearing a space with his arm, then ran back to return with bread and a bowl of salad. Two forks appeared out of his shirt pocket and they sat down to eat.

Lucy tasted the food nervously. Bits of fish. Smoked. Curry. Rice. Boiled eggs. She feared that the week's remains had been heated up in some kind of curry paste.

But two forkfuls satisfied her that it was remarkably tasty. "What is it?" she asked.

"Kedgeree."

"What's kedgeree?"

"The precise ingredients are a closely guarded secret, but I can tell you in general: rice, chopped egg, smoked haddock, and curry. I associate it with the Raj, brought back to Cheltenham and Bournemouth from India to take its place soon on the breakfast sideboards of English country houses, from where it descended to become a dish widely consumed by all classes."

"I'll look up the recipe."

"You won't find it, and if you do, it will be wrong. North American cookbooks suggest you can make it from cod and leave out the curry. The result is fishy rice. The real thing is only properly described in a book by Jane Grigson, called, I think, the *Book of English Cooking*. I'll look it up and write down the title for you, and then if you are just being polite, you can throw it into the lake on your way home. How's that? But if you are at all genuinely intrigued, then buy Mrs Grigson, or, at least, borrow her from the library."

Lucy smiled and nodded like a simpleton, taking in very little. What she was really watching and listening to was McSweeney's conversational style. As far as she could tell, he did not have an ordinary speaking voice, but chose a new diction for every remark. Thus in telling her about the objects on the table, he adopted the voice and posture of a stage conjuror, and for the recipe he seemed to be addressing a group of ladies at their monthly luncheon. It was not so broad as parody — he made no attempt at funny accents or imitations of well-known comic voices. He

gave a hint merely of how he should be read, sometimes by no more than changing the rhythm from the
normal. Thus the absence of the salt from the table
was treated with deep seriousness, in a tone suitable
for announcing the demise of close friend, whereas a
story of the actual death of an old friend was treated
like the bursting of a soap bubble. "Pop," he said.
"Off he went. Pop, just like that."

Lucy stayed for two hours, and much later she met
him twice more. Immediately she wanted to know what
was at the centre, driving his eccentricities, but though
she met one or two people who knew him, or of him,
she met no one for a long time who was curious about
him, the best summing him up as a "mildly odd bache-
lor," as if that explained anything. Eventually Lucy created her own understanding that McSweeney's style
was the result most of all of a fear of boredom, as he
tried to find for every remark, however trite, an empha-
sis that would bring it back to life. It was also a very
effective way, Lucy realized, of keeping others at a distance, of making intimacy difficult, but she could not
decide if that was a deliberate effect or just a by-prod-
uct of the playful manner which was employed for its
own sake.

Now Lucy finished her kedgeree and he took the
plate from her and considered where best to put it,
deciding finally on the floor. "And now," he
announced, "to the purpose of your visit." He
snapped forward and upright in his chair and rested
his chin on his laced fingers.

Lucy said, "Greta Golden."

"Is that the whole sentence? Which is the verb?" he
asked, a linguist faced with an interesting new language.

"It's the name of the person who referred me to you."

He tried it on his tongue several times, finally feeling a pronunciation he liked, and spoke her name as if he were announcing the winner of a competition. "Greta! Golden! Of course. Dear Greta. How is she? I haven't seen her for...." He made a show of counting on his fingers. "Twenty years. And now I remember what you said on the telephone. You want to know about her mother, wasn't that it? Some sort of class history you're writing?"

But while McSweeney was doing his impersonation of remembering how many years it was, Lucy saw something else going on. Not in his eyes: she had never seen anything in other people's eyes, whatever novelists said. Eyes were just eyes. It was faces that reacted, and now she saw something in McSweeney's face that suggested a mind concerned with more than just diverting boredom, a watchfulness, perhaps a wariness, pretending to forget temporarily what Lucy was there for in order to have room to think.

She said, "I mentioned the class picture. But it's not a class history I'm here about. Greta has received some news that makes her wonder if she knows the truth about her parentage."

"That's a portmanteau of a word. Shall we empty it out a bit? Her father and her mother?"

"Not her mother, no. Her father. She wants to know if there is any doubt about who that was."

McSweeney jumped up and did a large pacing walk, like a lecturer. "Has it ever occurred to you that in the history of science, technology, and all kinds of evolution, we always know who the father is — the father of photography, for example, or the father of wave theory — but we never know the mother. In life it is the reverse; we usually know the mother, but sometimes not the father."

As Lucy started to think whether this was true, she saw that it was another performance, designed to give him a chance to continue to watch her.

"You knew her mother, didn't you?"

"I can't deny it. Yes. I-knew-her-mother," as if he were reading words slowly appearing on a ticker tape. "Very slightly," he addded, in a normal manner.

"You know what I am trying to find out. Tell me what you think might help me." She decided on a touch of shock. "Did Greta's mother sleep around? If so, who with? Did you ever sleep with her?"

"Did-June-Turley-sleep-around?" McSweeney now addressed the jury. "Ignore the third question, ladies and gentlemen, as a vulgar solecism, a slip of the tongue by the witness. As to the first, what sort of evidence would be required to respond affirmatively to such a question? How to prove it? There was no gossip, no rumour, and on the basis of this witness's limited opportunity to observe the person in question, I would say not. From the time I knew her, and from the time Aubrey Golden appeared in her life, June Turley was deeply devoted to him. The marriage was inevitable, and any liaison with anyone else unthinkable."

"Did you go to June's wedding?"

"I wasn't invited."

"So you never saw June or Aubrey Golden socially again."

"I saw June frequently after she came back from England, but only because I had decided to be a big brother to Greta, which everyone seemed to approve of and I enjoyed. Her having no Papa, you see, and thus needing a male presence to avoid psychological deformity." He waited for her next question. "Is that it?"

"I came to find out what you knew of that crowd, June Turley's friends. Weren't you a part of it that winter?"

"They were all in graduate school. I was not. Our paths rarely crossed."

"But you say you became Greta's sort of uncle."

"I became Greta's sort of uncle, yes. But that doesn't signify. I like babies, and she was the only one around whose mother would trust me. So there you are. I asked for and was given a small responsibility for Greta's welfare and happiness. Ridiculous, no doubt, but true. That astonish you?"

"Not really. My landlord does the same thing for his niece."

"It's breaking out everywhere. Now we must scamper. It's time for you to run and catch the ferry." He put on a pith helmet that hung by the door, and picked up a walking stick, from which he extracted and examined the broken half of a thin sword and waved it in the air. "We shall make short work of them with this, I fancy," he said and hustled her out the door.

Although Lucy felt herself distinctly more sophisticated than when she had arrived in Toronto a year before from Longborough, she had not yet walked down the street with a sixty-five-year-old man wearing a tropical helmet, ragged shorts, clogs, and carrying a swordstick, but no one who McSweeney greeted in the short walk to the ferry seemed surprised, and that, she thought, spoke well for the island residents and accounted for why he lived there.

The ferry ride lasted just long enough for Lucy to realize that McSweeney had managed to avoid telling her anything about Greta's mother or her world by declaring his ignorance of her particular friends. But the least she might have expected was a bit of gossip about life in Yorkville before the arrival of the flower children, a culture she now suspected had left its mark on him. But no. He had said nothing that she didn't already know from Greta. But how had he become close enough to June Turley to be trusted with her child?

"I don't know," Greta said. "He was just always there. I never thought to ask where she met him, or how."

"I need another thread to pull. Isn't there someone still around from those days?"

"Not that I can think of. Ma cut them all off. Or left them behind."

"I suppose if I went to Winnipeg, I could get hold of a class picture from your mother's year ... ?"

"Hang on. Try Helen Biswas, she might know. She's been our store manager since before I can remember, and when I was growing up she used to look after me when Ma went on buying trips. Ma was powerfully attached to Helen, who was her sort of her guru. If she confided in anybody, it would be Helen. She's in the store tomorrow, in the afternoon. I'll call her to let her know you're coming. Yes, Helen's the one."

Chapter Eleven

Before Lucy tackled Helen Biswas, she made one more try at solving the case of the pharmacist's cash register. Although she could hardly be charged with the failure to find the thief, it irked her to have made such a feeble-seeming effort. She thought now that one man might have some more ideas, Michael Curnow, who specialized in security, and she called him in England.

He was delighted to hear from her, and responded confidently when she told him where the problem had got to. "It's all a blind," he said. "I'll tell you what he's up to, shall I? He's fiddling the tax people. See, if he declares a theft, then he doesn't have to pay tax on it, but he does have to show that he tried to do something about it. I bet you wrote a report that said just what he wanted. Something like, 'After a close examination of the tapes I did not observe any of your employees taking any money.' Right?"

"More or less."

"He's got what he wanted, then. He can tell the tax people now that the thief was scared away, see. Neat, isn't it? Your bloke is an artist. Usually they just arrange a bit of break-and-enter by a pal."

He kept Lucy chatting for a few minutes, then reluctantly pointed out that it was costing her long distance rates, and promised to phone her to find out what happened when she told the pharmacist.

Coopman was waiting for her call. "Figured it out, have you?" he asked.

"Your thief is too clever for me, Mr. Coopman. I *was* wondering, though, if the money is actually being taken from the cash register."

"I told you it was."

"But you find it missing when you are adding up the day's receipts, don't you? I mean, after the store is closed."

"That's when I balance. Sure."

"Do you leave the money on your desk, ever? When you aren't there?"

"Never."

"Then I know who is taking the money."

"Who?"

"You."

"I'm stealing from myself? Why would I do that?"

"It's a form of —" she searched for the word — "skimming. You declare you've been robbed and you keep the money."

"What's the point of stealing my own money?"

"Insurance?" This was something Lucy had thought of by herself.

"You can't insure money."

"Then it's the tax thing. You don't pay taxes on

money that's been stolen."

He barked, a laugh without any joy in it. "Nice try. But no. Sorry. I'll think about it, though. Sounds good. I'll ask my accountant if he sees any possibilities in it. He's a crook, too. The flaw is that to satisfy the revenue department I'd have to prove I had hired a detective who'd put in a camera, and run a police check on the girls. And I'd need a receipt for that, wouldn't I? No, all I ever do is shoplift from myself." He barked again. "You get one more try."

Embarrassed now, Lucy said, "Is this a game, Mr. Coopman? Are you really losing money from the till?"

He sighed. "No, it isn't a game, and yes, I really am losing money. So give it another whirl."

"You know the answer, though, don't you?"

"I'd like it to come from you. What did you do with the tapes, by the way?"

"I have them safe."

"You could drop them off at the store here."

"I'll keep them in the office."

"Okay." Then, after a pause, "Why?"

"Because they invade the privacy of one of your staff."

He laughed. "Sue-Ann? Those blouses she wears? You think she cares about privacy?" He laughed again. "Okay, then. You keep the tapes or throw them away. Then you can testify what a fine non-harassing employer I am. In the meantime, let me know if you get any other ideas."

They were eating at Obsession, a cafe on Harbord, Nina's choice, though Lucy was paying. "I want to consult you," Lucy had said.

"Johnny out tonight?" Nina asked.

"That's what I want to talk to you about. I didn't tell you everything that happened in New York."

"I feel like Anne Landers."

After the steaks and frites were disposed of, Lucy ordered a second glass of wine for them. "Wine is much cheaper in New York restaurants," she said. "Well, at the one I went to on Columbus Avenue, it was. I think Johnny's got another lady," she added.

Nina said, "Another lady? You make her sound as if she smells of talcum powder and lavender water. Screwing around, is he?"

"I think so." Lucy told her the story of the phone calls in New York.

"Have you asked him?"

"No."

"Why not?"

"I wanted to think about my response first. What if he says yes?"

"You want to know what you'll say? What will you say?"

"I don't know."

"What will you think?"

"I'll feel betrayed, I know that."

"What will you want to do about it?"

"I don't know. See, It's not like I'm his wife, is it?"

"What *is* it like?"

"Actually, it *is* like I'm his wife, and I've caught him being unfaithful, isn't it?"

"That's what it sounds like. So how do you feel?"

"I don't like it. If I were his wife, somehow it wouldn't be so bad. Husbands do it all the time, don't they? Though I don't think mine did. But what am *I* if Johnny's going to go after others? I thought we were — what do they call it — an item. Lovers don't have flings with other people, do they? That's just, as you say, screwing around. Wives can forgive a little fling. I can't. I feel betrayed."

Nina waited until another prompt seemed required. "It happens, Lucy."

"It's a first for me, but I'm new to this."

"You did have someone yourself after you left your husband, didn't you, before you met Johnny?"

"Oh, Ben, yes, my Trog." Lucy smiled, some of the misery going out of her. "But we weren't deceiving anyone else, and besides, we weren't an item — there must be a better term at my age. Ben just came by every two or three weeks and jumped my bones — there, that's the right phrase, isn't it? He was what I needed at the time to stop being respectable, to show I could do it, and he really *enjoyed* me. And I never saw him after I met Johnny. Just the once."

"Didn't he lie to you, though?"

"All the time. Pretended he was this and that. You know. But I never believed all those stories. I don't think he thought I did. The thing was, he didn't tell me any stories to cover up his other love life. The last thing he said at the racetrack was that *I* was his secret. Wasn't that nice? I can't manage this thing that Johnny's up to. Am I being old fashioned and silly? I feel like Rip Van Winkle. Totally out of my time."

Nina sipped her wine and waited. Then, when the pause had gone on long enough, she said, "Are you going to ask him?"

Lucy said, "I don't know. Will I be able to believe him, whatever he says? I feel uneasy. Is this the way I'm going to feel all the time now? It's not worth it. Is it?"

Nina sipped her wine. Lucy was talking to herself now.

Helen Biswas shook her head. "June never confided in me about her marriage," she said. "We talked about other things, a lot, because she had no family or other confidants, I think. We were on opposite sides of the fence in almost every way — spiritually, politically — except in our taste in pottery — but it didn't matter because we loved each other immediately."

Lucy was jolted by such apparently casual use of the word, but tried not to show it. Perhaps it was the way Indians talked. Helen Biswas was Indian, in Lucy's understanding, meaning her family originated from somewhere in the subcontinent, but Lucy couldn't remember if Greta had called her Indian, or Pakistani, or Sikh, or anything else. She was tall and fragile, with long thin hands and very narrow feet in beautiful leather shoes. She spoke exquisitely, laying out the skeletons of her words, so that, for instance, the word "coast" came out with almost no vowel but the "c" and the "t" were diamond clear.

"You weren't a pal of hers at Manitoba?"

"Oh, no. I came along about five years later when she needed someone for the store. I had been a good customer and it led her to ask me to keep my eye out for a likely employee, and I proposed myself."

"So you never knew any of her college friends?"

"No. The odd one used to come in from time to time to ask after her, but June kept her distance and they stopped appearing eventually."

"Why? Why did June put up a barrier?"

"Because she didn't want to be connected to them any more."

"Why? Did she have some deep dark secret she was afraid they might find out?"

"Perhaps. But whether that was the reason she cut off her old classmates, I don't know. Wait a minute. I know where you might start. One of her classmates is a librarian here at the Metro library. She persisted in trying to make contact with June longer than the others. She came in several times so I recognized her, and once, when I encountered her in the library building, we chatted for a few minutes about why June was so standoffish. She thought it was personal, but I felt free to tell her that I was sure it wasn't, that June had become very private, that was all. If you want to talk to her, you'll find her in the art department." She smiled. "You'd better be quick, she's close to retirement. Her name is Mary Disraeli."

Lucy introduced herself as a friend of Greta Golden who had been asked by Greta to put together some kind of family history. She was trying to find people who knew her mother, June Turley, in graduate school in the winter of 1957. Helen Biswas had mentioned her as a possible source.

The librarian said, "Sure, but I don't think I'm going to do you much good. I did graduate with her, but I hardly knew her. I took geography. Still, I thought we had a kind of acquaintanceship, at least, because we bumped into each other on campus here, but when I tried to keep up the connection she wasn't interested. See, we never saw much of each other socially in that year. We all moved in gangs: I was with the geography crowd until I took library science, and June was part of the history gang. They are the people you want to talk to. Hang on a minute." She disappeared into a back space and returned immediately with an album, bound in leather with a gold emblem on the cover. "Graduating class of '57," she said. "Here's our yearbook. Here's where we'll find them. Let's see if I can remember anyone who stayed in Toronto. A lot of us did."

Almost immediately she found the picture she was looking for. "Can I get a copy of this?" Lucy asked.

"Free to the trade." The librarian swivelled the picture around. "Let me see. There," She stabbed a finger at one of the faces. "Try her. She's around. Cathy Dickens. She works in the Robarts library. And him, of course. Derek Melvin. I'd forgotten him. He teaches history at Albert College here. Start with him. I know both of them so you can tell them I suggested their names. I'll call ahead and tell them you're coming by. What do you want? Facts? Gossip? Little anecdotes?" She picked up the phone and simultaneously turned to an assistant who had been waiting to talk to her, solved her problem, and then another from another assistant, then said to Lucy, "See if I can think of anyone else," and began dialling. Lucy moved away in case the librarian wanted to say something personal.

When she called Lucy back, she said, "Mission accomplished. They are waiting with bated breath."

"How do I get to these places? Albert College? And the library."

"Albert College is just off Bloor Street, you know? It's part of the university. Melvin's office is in the old section. You know where the Robarts library is, surely?"

"I've heard of it. I'll find it."

"Start with Melvin, then you can walk across Queen's Park to the Robarts. Good luck." She scratched her head with a pencil. "Be careful. These two people don't like each other much, so keep them separate, if you know what I mean."

The porter of Albert College directed her across a patch of grass to a grey stone building with leaded windows and a pointed doorway. Professor Melvin's office was on the second floor.

Never having experienced university life, Lucy was slightly and quaintly in awe of the title "Professor." She knew from her reading that these people could be spiteful, lecherous, unprincipled — in fact utterly unaffected by the liberal education they had received and were now dispensing, and at least one in every college was homicidal, but that was just in novels, and when she closed the book, the idea of a university returned, the word "professor" again implying a larger being than the ordinary, morally and intellectually.

She was glad therefore to find outside Professor Melvin's office a sign, "For Jesus' Sake Forbeare," in two-inch Gothic letters, on a piece of white cardboard.

She was not sure what the words meant, and did not remember having heard them before, but she was fairly sure the intent was facetious, which she derived in McLuhanesque fashion from the type used and the fact of the shirt card. Professor Melvin was clearly a wit, or at the very least, a joker, and she relaxed.

She knocked, and the door was flung open by a man with the face of a pig with a pair of steel-rimmed glasses set deep into the flesh, shouting "Can't you read?"

"Yes," she said. "But I don't know what it means. 'Be warned'?"

"That's it!" Melvin shouted. "You've solved the riddle of Portage Avenue. Why, when I specifically forbid it, do my students continue to badger me? Because they don't know what the words mean! The most famous gravestone in the language. But why should I think they would know that when they don't know anything else. Forbear means 'Refrain'."

"Forbear what? Refrain from what?"

"Forbear to do *anything*," he roared, but smiled, too. "Forbear to sell me anything, forbear to give me anything to mark, to ask me about the exam — forbear to do anything that will interfere with my afternoon nap. But since you are here, and I was warned to expect you, what can I do for you?" He stood back to let her in and pointed to a chair beside his desk.

Lucy sat down, took the picture out of the envelope and showed it to him.

"What's this?" He took it up and held it out. "The class of '57, by God. And there I am. I haven't seen this for years. Why are you showing it to me?"

"Is that you?"

"Not a bit. I am me. That is the youth I *was,* forty years ago, clean of limb, clear of eye, sweet of breath, stout of heart, and full of the dreams of youth. And look at me now. A nodding ruin." He stroked the shirt over his round belly, fondly. "Why are you tormenting me with this?"

Lucy leaned over the picture. "Didn't the librarian tell you? I am trying to find out about that one. She's dead now, but I want to talk to people who knew her then." She pointed to June Turley.

Some of the performer left him then. "Mary said you were researching a family history or memoir or something."

Lucy decided on a small shock, knowing that Greta would not mind. "Only in a way. June Turley left a daughter who is wondering now, because of certain recent events, whether she really is her father's daughter."

"Wondering if she really is her father's daughter!" Melvin roared. "Perfect! Art in the guise of life. Nineteenth century fiction is not my area but I'm familiar with the genre from teaching second year courses. Babies switched at birth, were they? Orphanages involved, no doubt? Beadles?" He laughed loudly but now Lucy saw he did not seem to have his heart in it. His eyes flickered as the thoughts chased themselves around inside his head.

"She came to Toronto in 1957 after graduation. She met her husband that winter and she became pregnant. Towards the end of her pregnancy, they went to England where the baby was born prematurely. When she came back, she didn't pick up with her old crowd, but started a new life with the baby.

She opened a shop, and then became a wholesaler of pottery. You probably know all this."

"So what can I do?" He took a piece of paper from his desk, smiled at what he read, and dropped it near the wastepaper basket. Then he drew a pile of mail towards him and began to slit the envelopes open with a paperknife. For the rest of their interview he dealt with his mail as he talked. Lucy presumed he had developed the habit while talking to students, but she found it rude.

The desk was heaped with paper, and the office festooned with rubbish. Piles of old essays covered a table and part of the floor; a second desk had a layer of paper several inches deep, some coffee cups, and an ancient manual typewriter. The walls were covered with clippings, pictures cut from magazines, and other objects — a paper kite and several cardboard theatrical masks among them — all joined in a collage-like way. The effect intended was that all this was subtly and meaningfully connected. The real effect on Lucy was to make her wish for a fire hose to wash the whole place down.

"Do you know who her friends were in Toronto when she first came east?" she asked.

"I knew her. I was here." He said this over his shoulder as he bent to read something on the floor.

"Were you ... friends?"

"We had been classmates in Manitoba. I knew her well. In Toronto, she was part of our gang in the King Cole Room at the Park Plaza on Friday nights. The Manitoba Mafia."

"The what?"

"It's what someone called us. In those days most Manitoba graduates tended to gravitate to Toronto for graduate work, whereas Saskatchewan and Alberta intellectuals dreamed of the spires of UBC. Hence there was a gang in Toronto every year from Manitoba. The Mafia."

"What about the students from the Maritimes? Where did they go?" Lucy asked, momentarily distracted from her task.

"I do remember one lad from New Brunswick. Big guy with thick yellow hair cut short and those orange work boots that became fashionable among undergraduates ten years later. We all assumed — no, let me be fair, *I* assumed, that he was a bit of a hick, but it turned out he was fluent in Anglo-Saxon, Latin, Old French and Old Norse — not fluent, literate. The priests in that New Brunswick lumber town he came from had trained him up like a greyhound to compete with the city boys in Toronto. He was their champion. It wasn't hard. The English majors from Manitoba could just about recognize Anglo-Saxon but that was all. But it is June Turley we were speaking of. She was very much a part of the scene that year. As I say, Fridays in the King Cole Room and a house party every Saturday. House party. Doesn't that sound grand? But how else are you going to label the fact that every Saturday you took twelve bottles of beer to someone's room, or apartment, and drank and ate and sang. Ask me about that."

"You did this every week? The same songs?"

"Yes, it was like a Victorian parlour evening, everyone doing a party piece. My own specialty was 'The Wild Colonial Boy.'" He looked at a letter he had just opened. "Now here's a former student wants to use me as a reference. Not a chance."

"Was he a poor student?"

"Actually, he was quite good. But did you know that these days if you write a reference for someone that is not cast in glowing terms you can be sued if the person gets hold of it and decides that its lukewarmness was the reason they didn't get the job?"

"I don't believe it."

"It has happened! Of course, referees always lied in the old days, but what we wrote was in code. We all knew what we meant. Now we don't. I fear, though, that you can be sued for *not* giving a reference at all, so now I just throw them away." He dropped the letter in the wastebasket.

"What did June Turley sing?"

"You keep dragging me back to her. My memories were just getting interesting. June didn't sing anything. Most of the girls didn't. Don't ask me why."

Probably because they were sober, Lucy thought. "Do you remember who else was there?"

"Milton. Milton Parrish. Lloyd Turner. Al Durstein. That was all the Manitobans in history, I think. And there was a man from Detroit who used to lead the singing in 'Michael, Row the Boat Ashore.' I heard he became head of Detroit airport."

"The girls?"

"Lloyd Turner and Al Durstein had wives. I didn't, nor did Milton or the Detroit man. As well there was a girl we brought with us from Winnipeg, Jennifer Newbold, and a girl called Brenda from Brandon, Manitoba. We called her Brenda from Brandon."

Lucy smiled to acknowledge the wit. "And Cathy Dickens?" she risked, watching for the effect of the name.

"You know the fair Cathy?" Melvin quietened down with the question.

"I'm going to see her next. Did June have a boyfriend?"

"She did indeed. A man called Golden. 'Golden Boy' we nicknamed him after the figure on the Manitoba legislative building. A little prairie joke."

"No others?"

"I see where you are going. No, so far as I know, June Turley had one boyfriend, Aubrey Golden, an Englishman, whom she married and by whom she had a daughter."

"When did you see her again?"

"I didn't actually, not for years. I moved away from that crowd. I believe they married that summer. The fair Cathy will tell you all, no doubt. That's about it from me, really. I could tell you a lot about those people as students — you know, how they handled themselves in the seminars and so forth. But that wouldn't help you, would it? Most of them didn't make it, you see."

"Didn't make what?"

"The necessary trade union paper for the academic life. The Ph.D. Most of them dropped out and went off to teach in community colleges." Melvin had run out of envelopes to open, and now began lifting piles of paper from his desk and dropping them in a different spot.

"You did, though."

"Luckily, I ran afoul of a very pompus old fart on the faculty — I made a joke which he took personally, and he withdrew his blessing from me. Really. Not in words, of course, but after that there was something missing when I was in his presence, the equivalent, I would think, for a believer, of God's grace. I was able to confirm that I wasn't being paranoid from another professor, a sort of mentor, who told me to switch graduate schools and arranged a fellowship to Yale." Recalling this, Melvin began to re-inflate. He picked up a pile of essays, looked at them consideringly, then dropped them in the wastepaper basket. "The deadline has passed," he announced, flourishing the words. His whole conversational style seemed more designed to execute flashy figures than to get from A to B.

"So you didn't stay close to your friends?"

"Apart from my wife, no. I lost contact with the rest."

"Did you know that June started up a business when she came back with the baby in 1959?"

"So I heard later. Did I ever make contact? No, because she made it clear that she wasn't interested in keeping in touch with me. I seem to remember hearing that the death of Aubrey Golden so soon after the birth of her daughter had unhinged her and she took a long time to glue herself together again. So perhaps there are lots of reasons. Others tried to seek her out and were also rebuffed. And now she's dead and relatives are quarrelling over the estate."

"Something like that. They haven't told me everything. Maybe her mother was rich — I mean June Turley's mother."

"June Turley's mother was the widow of a railroad man who lived in Transcona, not a very affluent town. An uncle of mine who also worked on the railroad rented a room from her. She died ten years ago."

"There don't seem to be any letters. Do you think June cut herself off from her?"

"More likely June was cut off when she got pregnant and had to get married. I think the family were Mennonites. And now I have to get some work done."

Lucy stood up, pleased to be dismissed. She was tired of Melvin in his performing mode, and glad that she didn't have to pay attention to him three times a week. "You've been very helpful," she said.

"Where to now?"

"Cathy Dickens." Lucy consulted her notebook. "Where is the Robarts library from here? Can I walk there?"

"Straight across the park, then along Harbord. About fifteen minutes."

As Lucy reached the door, Melvin added, "By the way, there was a sister, I think." He made an elaborate gesture of remembering. "Did you know?"

"Whose sister?"

"June's. A younger sibling by about two years. Not one of the crowd. Daisy. No, Rose. She dropped out of Manitoba in her second undergraduate year and came to Toronto to be with June. It's very vague. She wasn't around much. Soon she disappeared entirely. Perhaps La Dickens will know more." He turned away and Lucy left.

Chapter Twelve

And so it proved.

Lucy had no confidence in her taste in anything — art, architecture, music, painting, literature — she did not even know what she liked. Confronted with the demand to respond to an example of one of the higher arts she felt confusion and panic. Left to herself she was happy to wait until she felt something; her instincts told her not to close off her receptors, and her instincts were sound. Visiting the office of Nina, for example, who always had classical music playing quietly on her radio, she had learned the name of a terrific piece of music that she had overheard twice in one day — it was a Schubert piano trio — and asked Nina to write it down so that she could buy it when she bought a CD player. She liked Colville's landscapes immediately, and hoped to learn that it was right to do so, and she was trying to find a Canadian novelist on the approved list that she could read without having to sit up straight. But so far, when she wasn't reading crime fiction, she turned to Georgette Heyer, but without telling the world.

Nevertheless, with her first look at the Robarts library she felt the strength to oppose it, no matter who was listening. It was indefensible, a monstrosity of blackish-grey stone that looked like Darth Vader's castle, brutally contemptuous of its function in the history of truth and beauty.

Lucy tried to say something about it to Cathy Dickens, who she found in a room in the basement of the library, who just said, "I know. But I find it bracing after I've spent a couple of hours in Massey College."

Lucy made a mental note to find out what was wrong with Massey College, wherever that was, filed away the word "bracing", wondered if anything was indefensible, and took out her notebook.

"This is the museum, and I'm the curator," Cathy Dickens said. "In theory I'm retired, but I've come back to work on the archives and collections. It's what I was trained to do, not help undergraduates with their essays. Don't look at me like that. You're a librarian, too ..."

"I'm not a librarian," Lucy interjected. She had learned in Longborough that librarians were very touchy about helpers without diplomas using the title. There were librarians, library technicians, and dogsbodies. Lucy had once been a dogsbody.

"Mary Disraeli said you were."

"I worked in a library for a year. As a clerk, sort of."

"Did you, now? Well, anyway, I'm not putting down the students. How did we get on to this? What can I do for you?"

Cathy Dickens had black and grey hair arranged in a big scruffy knot at the back, so much hair escap-

ing the knot that it formed a cloud round her head.
Her eyes were blue, though slightly bloodshot, and
her face, though fresh and cheerful, looked battered
as if she had just showered after three rounds in the
ring. Her body was big and shapeless, clothed in a
sack-like garment and sandals.

"I need a puff," she said. "Let's go outside. Did
you bring a camera? I may be the last smoker left in
the University of Toronto library system. You should
get a picture."

"I'm sorry, I was staring. But I don't smoke. You
shouldn't, either."

"Did you come all the way from the Metro
Library to tell me that? That's kind of you. I don't
take care of myself in a lot of other ways, but I'm still
here. Now. Mary Disraeli called. Said you seemed
harmless. You look it. What do you want to know?"
They were outside now, sitting on the stone wall
beside the library steps. Lucy told her.

"And who gives you the right to ask? Sorry, you
told me — Greta Golden. June's daughter. Well, I
don't know what I can tell you."

"I've already talked to Professor Melvin."

"That fraudulent old mountebank. He was an asshole back then, too. What did he tell you?"

"He told me about the Manitoba Mafia, how you
all used to party on Saturday nights."

"Did he tell you who were in this gang?"

Lucy consulted her notebook and read off the
names. The woman listened to the roll call, looking
bleak. "June Turley, Aubrey Golden, Al Durstein — all
dead," she said. "Yes, I'm still in touch with Brenda.
We exchange Christmas cards. "If she comes to Toron-

to we have dinner. So why are we talking? What do you want to know?"

"I'm not sure. Yes, I am. As far as you know, was Aubrey Golden her only lover?"

"As far as I know Aubrey was her only *boyfriend*. I don't know if they were lovers." She lit up as she spoke, then went into a fit of coughing that made Lucy want to hold her until it stopped. She looked through her notes to let the woman calm down. "Professor Melvin said that June had a young sister," she said. "Did you meet her?"

"He remembered Rose, did he? I've almost forgotten her myself, but it all comes back vividly now. Did he mention anyone else, not one of the mafia? I'm not surprised. It's all part of the same memory, though. Let me describe one scene to you." A much smaller fit of coughing now seemed to end the attack for the present.

"Imagine, if you can, an apartment on Cumberland Street, where it meets Avenue Road, across from the church. The block is long gone, torn down like much of the village after the hippies were forced out by the rents in the seventies. This was before the hippies arrived, before the Beatles, even. There was a nice old apartment block at the end of the street, and some students shared one of the apartments. On this Saturday night, these students hosted the moveable feast — you know, made the chili and salad. Now, everything was going as merrily as a wedding bell — someone was singing — then crash! Our hero Derek Melvin comes reeling down the hall clutching his face which was bloody from a cut under one eye. And then another man appeared, a stranger to us, and the two of them started to scuffle. Melvin was clearly no match for the stranger, though neither of them were what you would call *fighters,* and a couple of the boys grabbed him while others persuaded Melvin to leave. He didn't take much urging." A laugh turned into a cough which became a paroxysm. When it subsided she lit another cigarette and continued. "I don't remember seeing him after that, there or at any later party." Each short sentence now had to wait for a gasp of breath. "A little while later, June announced that the party was over. Later we learned that they were fighting over Rose who was somewhere around. So you see, that's why our Melvin remembered that June's sister was there."

"He never mentioned you until I did."

"Did he not? I'm not surprised. We don't socialize, you see, which is hard when you are connected to the same institution. I haven't even seen him on the street for about a year."

"But what happened? Did Rose ever appear?"

"The thing is, talking about it afterwards — and we sure as hell *did* talk about it afterwards, none of us could remember Rose being at the party. As far as we could remember, the stranger had appeared on his own, and got into a fight with Melvin. They must have started being rivals off-stage."

"Did you learn who the stranger was? Rose's boyfriend?"

"His name stuck. Sweeney. Like in Sweeney the barber."

Close enough, Lucy thought. "What happened to the sister?"

"I've no idea. She just disappeared. Whether she left Toronto or Canada, even, I don't know. I never saw her again. She didn't keep up with us. No, that's not accurate; the gang didn't exist any more, but even so, some of us stayed in touch. But the only one whose whereabouts I know of now is Melvin, and I have to cross myself whenever I go past his college."

"Is he so bad?" Lucy had stopped pretending to take notes. Cathy Dickens' opinion of Melvin was clearly informed by a distorting animus, and Lucy was curious to know its roots.

"Did you meet his wife?" Dickens asked.

"Why would his wife be in his office?"

"Right. She stays home. Sits behind drawn curtains and drinks. She is a total alchoholic, driven mad by him."

"You make it sound like one of those American novels they used to make into films for Ronald Reagan. There's a word."

"Gothic?"

"I think that's it. I never took any courses."

"It'll do."

"How did he make her alchoholic?"

"By marrying her. She was a very sweet girl before she met him. Melvin wheels her out from time to time for state occasions, to meet the new chancellor, for example, and she hangs on to a sober act for as long as it takes, then he sends her home. The public story is that she has chronic fatigue syndrome."

"Why is it *his* fault?" A note of irritation crept into Lucy's voice in response to this black-and-white tale.

"I'm telling you how it is. She inherited a lot of money, which is the only reason he keeps her."

"What went wrong?"

"Nothing ever went right." She said this belligerently, in a way to challenge any doubter, but when Lucy made no comment, she added, "You see, these were the sixties, and Melvin was one of those professors from the outside world who brought the news of the revolution from New Haven to Toronto. He was a charismatic figure in an ersatz sort of way; 'the guru of the tundra.' He had no difficulty plundering his female students."

"Including some you knew?"

"Including one I knew. How did you guess?"

"You're laying it on a bit strong."

"Am I? Melvin *is* a bastard, believe me. What else can I tell you?"

"Who else stayed behind in Toronto who might have known June?"

She shook her head. "Once or twice in the next decade I sought June out at her shop, first in a little basement on Cumberland, then the showroom on Davenport. In the beginning there was just her and the baby. She was the first person of our generation I knew to take her baby to work. Some of the customers were shocked. Luckily Greta was a good baby and in a year June had the business up and running, so she could probably afford a daycare. I don't know. I really lost track of her, or rather — because I did know where the shop was — I took her hint and stopped calling for a long while.

"The last time I went in was seven or eight years ago. The Good Earth was now at least three times the size of the first store. It was obvious she was doing well. I'm not much for all that *House and Garden* shit, but I could tell this was the right stuff. To cut a long story short, I asked if she was there. I mean, what the hell, we used to be pals. She wrote all my philosophy essays in third year. Where was I — oh yes, the woman running the store said June was hardly ever there. Apparently she had expanded, but not sideways, into a chain, but upwards, into the wholesale end. Now she travelled around buying merchandise for other people's stores. Very successfully, too. She kept the store, because retailers she sold to liked to tell their customers in Atikokan that the pots were the same ones carried by The Good Earth in Toronto. As I say, it was now a kind of showroom, but it still sold the stuff. Is it still there?"

"Her daughter keeps it going. But what happened to June Golden to make her cut herself off like that?"

"Everyone has a theory, among those who knew her. Grief is a popular one. The loss of a husband so young. Another one that had some vogue for a while was that she had become lesbian, and didn't want to spend her time explaining herself to her old acquaintances. That was 1959, and it was much easier not to leave the closet than it is now."

"Did you think so?"

"Not then, not now. Take my word for it, she was quite straight." Dickens took a deep drag of her cigarette and threw the butt away. "She didn't become a recluse, by the way. She was quite comfortable in the retail scene, first among the flower children when the stuff she sold fitted the back-to-nature crowd, then by the time Yorkville turned into a kind of outlet mall for the European luxury stores like Hermes and those English shirtmakers, she was ready for that. She just charged more." The librarian was dreaming now, enjoying the memory. "A lot of people have taken against Yorkville, but it will always be a stop-off point for people like me. The area is still full of ghosts. If I sit in the Coffee Mill long enough I'm bound to see some-one I knew, or knew of."

"Did anyone see or hear more of the young sister?"

"No, she *did* disappear. But that may be too strong a word. She wasn't part of our crowd so maybe she just went off and found her own world. That's what people do when they grow up. Don't they?"

"Usually. But what would you say now about June, after nearly forty years?"

"My guess, without the slightest evidence, is that a couple of things happened. First of all, she didn't want to talk about her husband's death. Then I sus-pect she quarrelled with her mother. There was a rumour that her mother judged her for having the baby too early. The story was that the two of them had a huge row with June refusing to be chastised, and they never spoke again.

"You have to realize that what I'm telling you is legend, probably one-tenth true; that's what the story of June has become to us who used to know her. I've stayed in touch with a couple of them and every few years we add another sentence to the leg-end of June Turley. Someone claimed to have seen her in the first-class section of the plane going to Costa Rica, with a latin type. Unfortunately for that story there is no first-class section on that plane. When the story that she was killed made the papers, we wanted to acknowledge it, but no one really knew her daughter. The connection was very faint by then.

"You see what I mean — the fence going up, the success, make her story intriguing and interesting, to us, anyway — I suppose every group has someone like June — but not really remarkable. I haven't thought about her for years, because I haven't thought about that scene for a long time. I've lost touch with most of the people I knew then. How many friends do you have from the old days?"

"I never went to university. Is any of what you've been telling me confidential?"

The woman considered Lucy for several seconds. "I have no secrets. Everyone knows what I think about Melvin. Where to now?"

"Back to Mary Disraeli. I have some better questions to ask her now."

The librarian shrugged, slightly disconcerted. "Mary's a good sort. She'll probably defend Melvin. But ask away."

Mary Disraeli said, "Did she really know you were going to ask me? Just a minute." She turned and dialled a number. "Cathy," she said, looking at Lucy as she spoke. "This lady is back and says you know that she will ask me to verify your story. You know I've always thought you are totally unfair, and I'll tell her why. You knew that. Yes, all right, let's get together soon."

She turned to face Lucy. "Cathy tells everyone that Melvin's lechery has made his wife a recluse and an alchoholic. That's simply not true. Melvin would sue Cathy if he wasn't frightened of her. He is not much of a lech, never was, and his wife was an alchoholic in high school, with a mickey of rye in her locker in Grade Twelve. She inherited her addiction."

"Cathy said Melvin married her for her money."

"She had no money. Her father's had all been drunk, and the mother never had any. Melvin doted on the girl. He was totally and utterly in love with her, and for all I know, still is. Professor Melvin is a blowhard, a fool, and a posturer, but he doesn't rape his students and he has always been a nurse to a sick wife."

"If she knew you would deny her version, then why did she tell it like that?"

"You'll need a psychologist to sort that one out. Maybe it gives her a chance to say what she likes about Melvin without worrying about being fair. She loathes him. No one who knows her listens to her, but an outsider might be impressed."

"But why is she so down on him? Do I need a psychologist for that, too? Or were they mixed up with each other and he betrayed her?"

"Betrayed her? How? Oh, I see. No. They were never entangled, no. Actually, I'll tell you, because it won't make the slightest difference to your investigation, and Cathy would deny it, anyway, but it has to do with the difference between men and women students in Toronto then. She was in a class with Melvin in graduate school. She's right that Melvin has a B-plus brain; hers is or was A-plus when she was a student. So, came the day that she was planning her future; Melvin had already wangled a fancy scholarship to Yale ..."

"He told me he'd run afoul of a professor. A pompous old fart, he called him."

"I've heard that story, too. But the real point is that after they fixed Melvin up with a PhD program

at Yale, they told Cathy, or rather this particular professor told Cathy, that she might as well drop out
because he didn't believe in recommending women
for anything beyond the MA. He thought women academics were lacking in decorum, ought to get married. In those days you could expound a view like that
at the head table of any Toronto college. So she
dropped out, but she never got over the fact that a
second-rater like Melvin could be preferred over her.
But she shouldn't keep telling stories about him."

"What about this fight he got into? Did that
happen?"

"I know the story he tells, but I wasn't there.
You'll have to find someone who was."

Chapter Thirteen

Greta's company occupied space on the ground floor of a warehouse at Adelaide and Spadina, and Greta suggested that they meet in the coffee bar on the same floor. "It's only just opened, so we are all trying to bring it business to keep it here."

Lucy gave Greta an account of what she had learned so far and asked about her mother's sister.

Greta said, "I meant to mention her when we were talking about great uncles and whatnot. She disappeared before I was born. I don't think she even went to the wedding. My mother never talked about her. If I asked her, she just said her sister had cut herself off. I've never given her much thought — just an aunt I was supposed to have had once, who didn't get along with my mother." She drank some carrot juice and made a face. "My guess is that she is in Europe somewhere now. Certainly not in Canada, or she would have seen the report of Mother's death. 'Canadian woman shot in Florida motel' was a big story for a couple of weeks, and surely she would have responded. Made sure I was all right. The only one who did get in touch was Jim McSweeney from the island. What's more likely, if she's still alive, is that she doesn't know her sister is dead. Even if she lives in England, the death of a Canadian woman in Florida isn't likely to make *The Daily Mirror,* is it?

She looked up. In the doorway a young woman was signalling agitatedly. Greta pointed at her watch to indicate she would be there shortly. "Crisis," she said. "Got to go soon. Meanwhile *I've* been busy. I've talked to three other people I would call mother's most recent friends, including, my dear, her last lover. Isn't that something? I had no idea that they were lovers. I had no idea back then that people that age *had* lovers. He was her closest friend's husband, and they used to meet once a week in a little room behind his shop."

"What kind of shop?"

"Antique books. On King Street. This affair lasted more than twenty years, from the time my mother was about my age, until she died. Once a week in a little room behind the shop. God. She visited him like she visited a masseur."

"For her health?"

"Exactly. No, that's not fair. Mr. Lockhart got quite — well — moved, when we were talking about her. I asked him if there was ever any chance that he might have left his wife and married my mother, and he said he wanted to, and asked her more than once. His wife's dead now — I gather the marriage wasn't very lively, and yet there was no question of his leaving. Apparently Ma always said that if he breathed a word about them, to his wife or anyone else, she would make his life absolute bloody hell. She didn't say how, but he believed her; I think she must have been a control freak."

"And what's that?" Lucy had a lot of catching up to do in the area of the vocabulary of popular psychology. "What's a control freak?"

"Someone who has to be in charge. You know the kind."

"I married one, I think. But I would say that keeping control of the situation was your mother's way of keeping it a secret. What's the word for that?"

"I don't know. Secretive? You think that's all it amounted to? This family of mine is turning out to be a great one for secrets."

"Maybe she just wanted to stay friends with his wife," Lucy suggested. "What about the other people you talked to?"

"Carole Lucas played tennis with her for years and knows nothing about her past; I asked her to tell me everything she could remember she had heard about mother all the way back to her college days. It took about two minutes. Carole knew she had been to the University of Manitoba, but that was all. She never met a single friend of mother's from the old days.

"It was exactly the same story with the other one. Louise Thomas, another tennis player. She was the only one with a bit of gossip that she thought might help, though only to make a connection I already knew about. She met up with Mother once on the ferry to Ward's Island. Mother said she was visiting someone she knew who worked in publishing. Louise, of course, assumed that Mama was having an affair and did a little rooting around among her friends on the island, and they came up with Jim McSweeney."

"The librarian mentioned him, too. Not like that, just as someone who once appeared in the winter of '57. I have to talk to him again. Did *you* ever visit him on the island?"

"I remember once as a young girl, going with my mother. Just once. And then, later, when I was eighteen or nineteen, a boyfriend and I took a day trip over to the island, and I thought to call in on him. But he was very pissed off about it. Not welcoming. In fact he took me aside to say I must never drop in on people without warning, especially him. So I never did again. Poor fellow. He probably had a woman in the bedroom and thought I would be shocked."

"Where does he come from?"

"Somewhere in England originally. Helen Biswas says he has an upper class accent. She jokes that he's the son of a lord, like Tarzan. He *is* very private."

"Do you think he could have been a ... lover?"

"You mean Mama was the woman in his bedroom? No, I don't think so. She was agreeable to him when he came to the shop with presents for me, and they were very comfortable together, like second cousins who like each other. I think she was grateful for his attention to me."

When she called him, McSweeney sounded perfectly happy to speak to Lucy again. "But come in person," he said. "I only use the telephone for messages."

So she travelled back on the ferry and he met her at the dock and took her to the little café for tea. "The treasure who cleans my house comes today," he explained. "She refuses to work with me in the house."

Lucy was struck by the search McSweeney must have undergone to find a cleaning lady who would set foot in the old curiosity shop he called a home. "Where did you find her?" she asked." Did you have any problem getting someone to come over from Toronto?"

"Indeed I did. Cleaning ladies are afraid of crossing water, did you know? The one or two that did come, did not return. And then I found my treasure, Deirdre, a young lady who lives on the island and is attempting to support herself in a minimal fashion while she writes her first novel. I see in your eyes you are still curious. I pay her twenty dollars an hour for four hours every other week, and with that and I think two other cleaning jobs she lives in a tiny house on the island and writes her novel."

"Can she clean the house in four hours every two weeks?"

"Eventually. Bit by bit. She moves steadily forward, lifting, dusting, polishing, you know, and remembers how far she has got, so that the next time she comes back, she can start in where she left off."

"Lucky you, and lucky her, I guess. Sounds like you suit each other."

"Perfectly. Now, what new enquiries are under way?"

"I've been talking to some people who knew June Turley back in 1957."

"Ah-ha!" He swiveled suddenly in his chair in a "Got it!" gesture. "And what did these fifty-seveners have to say?"

"You *were* part of the crowd that socialized on Saturday nights that winter."

"How that trips off the tongue," he said, admiringly. "No, I wasn't."

"But you were at one party, at least."

"One party, yes. At most as well as at least."

"You got into a fight, with a man named Melvin."

"Not a fight. I hit him. I drew back my right arm and hit him square in the mush, the only time I have ever done that, and very satisfying it was, though I was sorry afterwards."

"Why?"

"Why what? Which part are you querying?"

"All of it. Why did you hit him and why were you sorry afterwards?"

"All this was a long time ago, I remember, but ..."

"But you remember being sorry."

"All right. I hit him because I didn't like him. So I was sorry after I hit him because you shouldn't go around hitting people you don't like." He wagged a finger, a chiding parent. "But you know, until then I didn't know I knew how to hit. Some atavistic knowledge lurking in the genes behind this refined exterior. I remember, too, to my shame, that I wanted to hit him again. Not that I had anything against him but I'd enjoyed it so much the first time. Blood lust, you see. You have to be on the watch for it."

"What were you doing at the party, if you weren't a regular?"

"It was the times. One heard of a party, one went. Six beers got you in."

Lucy said, "That was after, surely, in the sixties. I've been getting a lot of history lessons lately. No one else has mentioned gatecrashers at the parties that winter. In fact, they remember you as a stranger, but not a gatecrasher."

McSweeney looked disconsolate and repeated the game of counting on his fingers. "You are quite right. I was invited."

"Who by?"

"Greta's mother's sister, as I remember. Rose."

"But she wasn't a regular at these parties, either, was she?"

"I don't know. I wasn't there."

"Were you close to Rose Turley?"

"You may cease your speculation on that point." This was said in the unfraught voice of a parent resisting a child's efforts to know something beyond its years.

"Sorry, but I'd still like to know what the fight was about. Was it over Rose?"

"That was the immediate cause, but the first and final cause was that I didn't like him."

"*Was* it over him pestering Rose?"

"'His', not 'him.' If you insist, then yes, but I would have hit him whoever he was pestering. It seemed clear to me that he *was*. Alone, leaning over a girl who had had too much to drink, lying on a couch in disordered clothing. It looked to me like a genre painting. Ruin, or some such. But I should have enquired because Rose assured me vehemently, then and later, that she was untouched by Melvin. But as I say, I was glad I had hit him before I had enquired."

Lucy was becoming aware that McSweeney's conversational style, while primarily devised to avoid boredom, was also ideal for allowing him not to let slip anything he didn't want to reveal. Nevertheless, what she overheard in all this was not the story of the accusation of Melvin and his acquittal, but of McSweeney's attachment to Rose Turley.

"What happened to her?"

"She went away."

"Where?"

"I didn't follow her."

"Didn't her sister say anything about where she went? Didn't anybody? And are you going to make me natter along like this all afternoon? Did you ever see that crowd again? Tell me the rest."

"There is no 'rest,' I'm afraid. Apart from what I told you in our conversation recently. The sister went away, and I was never invited to another party."

"But you stayed a friend of June's and behaved like an uncle to Greta when she was growing up."

"I needed a child to buy treats for, she needed a father figure. We were made for each other. And now, what's *your* next move, Inspector?"

"That's up to Greta. She was born in England. Perhaps I should go over there, see if anyone remembers her."

Twice Lucy had answered the phone and been hung up on. Once would not have been significant; twice in the space of two days was memorable. She mentioned the second call to Johnny who said it was probably some woman who was in love with him whose voice Lucy might have recognized, and he laughed.

It was a good answer, mainly because it was clever. But when the third call came, he answered the phone himself, listened for a moment, then said, "You have the wrong number," slowly and clearly, and put the phone down. When she asked him who they wanted — had he forgotten she used to be Mrs. Brenner? — he looked confused, said "What?" then, "I don't know. Lenny. Guy wanted to speak to Lenny," and she knew he was lying.

Her husband had often refused to tell her why he was doing something, like switching off the television, but that was his way of letting her know he was protecting her from filth of some kind, his brand of paternalism. He had no need to tell lies. This was different. Lucy felt her world had been infected.

She asked Nina again, who said, "If I were you I would decide what you want to do about it, then I wouldn't do it yet. There are other possibilities you might want to eliminate. A lot of women look twice at your Johnny Comstock, and one of them might have flirted a little with him one night in New York, and it got out of hand. Now he's being chased, and he doesn't want to tell you about her."

"You think he had a whatdoyoucallit, a one night stand? And that's all right these days, is it?"

But Nina was not to be drawn. "Maybe a bookie is trying to collect."

But Johnny never bet.

Chapter Fourteen

"There aren't any diaries, of course." Lucy swallowed a piece of croissant. "This is good," she said.

Greta had invited her for breakfast at Patachou, the French café at the end of her street.

"The best in Toronto. So is their bread. No, there isn't a goddamn thing except for what you've already seen, a business appointment book for her last year, and the year before, and her income tax records. No letters, no postcards, no memorabilia, nothing."

"The clue is that there is no clue. It's getting obvious that when your mother came back from England she made every effort to wipe out her past. She cut herself off from old friends, never told new friends anything about her past — systematically shredded the files on herself."

"But people knew who she was. She didn't change her name and wear a wig and dark glasses or anything."

"She didn't have to. Her old crowd simply lost touch with her. They knew about her store, but they got a cool welcome when they called, so they didn't call again."

"So why did Ma drop out? Not because she was feeling anti-social, because after she dropped out she dropped in — put together a new circle of friends and lived a perfectly normal life, if you don't count the bookseller's back room. I was there. She was a wonderful mother to me, doing all the things mothers are supposed to do, but mostly letting me use the shop first as a playpen, then as a playroom. Not just Jim McSweeney, but half Yorkville played Auntie and Uncle. It was like a Frank Capra movie. And Ma never pushed me behind the counter. I had to *ask* her if I could work in the store. Then it turned out I have a good eye, and I went along with her on one or two buying trips. To Oaxaca in Mexico once, and to Belize."

The waitress appeared between them. "More coffee?"

Lucy nodded, pushing her empty cup forward. "And did you never ask about her family, your grandparents?"

"Of course I did. I wanted a grandad like everyone else and an apple-cheeked old granny, and aunts and uncles, but she just told me that my grandad was dead before I was born, and my granny about seven years later. I remember her telling me she had a sister, but she had gone away, no one knew where. She was very offhand about my missing relatives, so I didn't work up any excitement about them until now."

"What did she tell you about your father's people?"

"I just understood my father had come over from England after his parents died, and there were no brothers or sisters there, either. We know different now, don't we? I wonder why she didn't just shrug them off, too, instead of pretending they didn't exist?"

"Because she didn't know? Because he didn't tell her?"

"Of course, that's it! It wouldn't be like her to lie, but for all we know he simply shucked off his family when he stepped on the boat, sort of dropped them overboard."

"Was he in graduate school with the rest of them?"

"Oh, no, no. He was a bookkeeper of some kind. My mother met him when they were both working at one of those agencies for temporary clerical help."

Lucy said, "It's still hard to understand what these relatives of yours in England are after. I mean, even if your father —"

"Wasn't my father, just someone my mother married when she found she was carrying me. Legally he was, though, so there's no grounds for disputing the will. As far as the law is concerned, that's that. But they haven't removed their objection. They aren't ready to give up all that money without an argument."

Lucy said, "It just sounds like your English relatives are being greedy. Have you asked your lawyer what chance they have?"

"Not a hope in hell, he says, and if they've consulted a lawyer at all he will tell them so."

"Then why not let the lawyers take care of it? Legally the money's yours, and it certainly doesn't belong to them. Just by contesting your share, they've lost the right to it. Not legally, but — they sound like terrible people."

"They do, don't they? And yet."

"What?"

"I'd still like to know the whole story. I think my English relatives are being uncommonly vicious and working against their own interest, or ..."

"You want me to say 'or what?'"

"I want you to say that they might just know something we don't."

"Like what?"

"Try this: suppose they know my father was sterile?"

"How would they know that and how would you find it out?"

"From a doctor. If he had a certain kind of mumps as a child, that would do it. There are probably a dozen other causes. Some disease he caught in his teens he never told anyone here about."

"You'll never know until these relatives turn up in court."

"Possibly. And even then it won't do them any good. But in those days in Canada you had to have a blood test before you married to show you didn't have syphilis. Isn't it possible that the doctor who took his blood sample would have discovered this other thing?"

"Greta, you're making this up."

"I've called up everyone I know to see if anyone can remember a doctor that my parents might have gone to. There might be a record still."

"From forty years ago?"

"What happens to a doctor's records when he gives up his practice? I'm going to find out as soon as I know his name. *I want to know who my father was!*"

Two women at the next table pretended not to be listening. Lucy said, "Let's take our coffee outside. It's still warm enough."

Resettled at a sidewalk table, Lucy began. "Let me play devil's thing, you know. First of all Aubrey Golden was a liar. That we know. So let me tell you what my landlord would do with this. My landlord. He makes up plots, pretends I'm the expert. I'll explain later, but what he would say is that because Aubrey Golden was a liar, we can't know anything for sure. For example, the family story is that he came over, spent two years in Edmonton, then moved to Toronto, where he met your mother. Right? Maybe he was already married."

"A bigamist? Then his marriage to my mother woudn't be legal, would it, so I wouldn't be his heir."

"Then again, maybe he — the man your mother married — was an imposter. Maybe he knew that Aubrey Golden had died in an avalanche in the Rockies and decided to adopt his identity. Used to happen all the time in the books I read. Then somehow his double life caught up with him in Cornwall. Maybe after he died. I mean, maybe when the local paper published a picture of the dead man someone came forward and said, 'That's not the Aubrey Golden I knew.' See? The possibilities are endless."

Greta was smiling now. "What a lovely load of balls. But I would like to find out about Aubrey Golden. Could you have a go? Find out what the hell happened on December 2, 1958, and who the actors were?"

"When?"

"My birth date."

Lucy considered. It was a foolish escapade, and she would do her duty to her client by telling her so once more and then she would go. It suited exactly her wish to get away from Toronto for a few days and consider her own situation. "It's your money," she said. "But I think you are wasting it."

"Five hundred a day," Greta said, "Plus expenses." She stood up and began to look for money for the bill.

"Can I ask you a personal question?" Lucy asked.

Greta looked at her warily.

"How much rent do you pay for your apartment?"

"You looking for an apartment?"

"I may be. I like yours."

Greta shook her head. "It's a condo. I paid a hundred and eighty thousand two years ago." She regarded Lucy appraisingly.

"Are there any left?"

Greta looked surprised. "No, but people do leave. Want me to call you up if I hear of anything?"

"If you wouldn't mind me as a neighbour."

"Why should I? It's friends, his and mine, I have to keep out. Okay. I'll keep my ears open. Let me know if you change your mind." She pushed her chair against the table. "Do you think it will suit him?" she asked.

"Who?"

Greta blushed. "I'm sorry. I understood you were part of ... a pair."

"From Nina?"

"She wasn't gossiping. I wheedled it out of her. I was curious, that's all. Toronto's just a village, you know."

Lucy shook her head. "Don't worry about it. You're right, though. It wouldn't suit him. But it might suit me."

"I'm going to rush right over and tell Nina what you said. 'Bye."

To Johnny, she said, "I'm going to England to make some enquiries for Greta Golden. Look up her birth records, that sort of thing. Counting jet lag and a couple of days sightseeing in London, I think I might be away for a week or ten days. Do you mind?"

"Whereabouts in England?"

"Cornwall, mostly."

He shook his head. "No real racing there. Just steeplechasing. Still ..." He looked as if he was considering it.

"You want to come?"

"There's a guy at the stables who is putting together a little tour of some racecourses in England. I don't know the itinerary, or if there's still room."

"When will you know?"

"Not until you've gone."

"I'll be in London for two days, then I'm going up to Cornwall. After that, I'm not sure."

"*Down* to Cornwall. *Up* to London. Call me when you've finished just in case we could meet up. Send me a fax when you know where you'll be. And let me know when you're coming back."

Of course, Lucy thought, the misery returning. Give you plenty of warning.

Chapter Fifteen

There was just the pharmacist left, but Lucy did not have much hope of finding a solution to that little puzzle.

She stopped by the office to pick up her heavy shoes, and to let Peter know that she would be away for a few days. She liked him to check on her office when she was gone for more than a day, and he liked to sit in her chair and talk to Nina on the phone while he waved to her through the window.

He accepted the assignment, barely listening. "You were right," he said. "But it didn't work out. Those two guys drove down to Cherry Beach and dumped the body, but on their way back that cop car appeared and wanted to know why they were driving around that area. Remember those cops? Right. So now they had to identify themselves, the whole thing. So when the cops drove off, they had to pick the body out of the lake and put it back in the trunk because otherwise, when the body is found, the cops will remember who they saw nearby and ..."

"So all they have to do is find somewhere else to get rid of the body."

Peter stared at her. "It can't be that simple. I had it all worked out." Then as she was moving away, he said, quickly, "'Ere's another one, a quickie. I haven't got *it* all worked out yet, but there's this barber accused of murdering someone by cutting 'is throat. But only a right-'anded guy could have made that particular throat cut, so they let this guy go because there's a cop at the station oo's been going to this same barber for twenty years and swears 'e's left-handed. But then the clever detective — you, maybe — points out that the policeman 'as only ever seen the barber's hands in the mirror and therefore, etc. etc. What do you think?"

"It needs spinning out."

"I got the idea from your mirror."

Lucy said, "Of course. That's what the poem means. She died of grief when she saw that Lancelot was left-handed. In those days that was very sinister. Now leave me alone. I have to call the pharmacist, just to get him off my mind."

"You caught the thief?"

"No. We've got videotape of everyone who uses the till, the two girls and another one occasionally, and none of them are trying to steal money. Either they know when he's pressing the button, or there's someone else ... Oh, Jesus. Of course. Leave me alone, Peter."

He told her to say no more over the phone, that he would come to her office right away.

"You knew it was your wife, didn't you?" Lucy

said, when he sat down. "You never switched on the camera when she was near the register."

"I didn't want a picture of her stealing from me. I didn't want anyone to see pictures like that, or her to find they exist."

"But you knew it was her before you hired me."

"I was pretty sure."

"Then why did we tape the others?"

"To be fair to everybody. I wanted to make sure it was just her. I had to prove they *weren't* stealing. Now I know. It's all her."

"You seemed to be kind of enjoying it, if you ask me. Watching me try to catch her."

"I did enjoy the stuff you made up about me stealing from myself. My acountant says I'd never get away with it. Lots try, he says. But I was just postponing the inevitable. And the next bit's no fun, either."

"You won't need me anymore."

"I need a marriage counsellor. Know any?"

Lucy understood that the man was simply revealing a sadness, not making a real request for a recommendation. She said, "Have you thought about why she is stealing?"

"It makes no sense. She can have anything she wants. All she has to do is ask."

"But she does have to ask."

"Or steal, I guess. What's the point of this?"

"Does she have any money you don't know about?"

"I hope not. Should she?" The tone was rhetorical, derisive.

This was something Lucy thought she knew something about. "Of course she should. Give her an allowance. Put her on the payroll."

"But I'd know about that, wouldn't I?"

"Not if she saved it for a couple of months."

"You mean don't tell her I know she's stealing, but give her some money?"

"It's worth a try."

"What if she carries on stealing?"

"Give her a raise."

He laughed. "And if it still doesn't work? I just have a pharmacy, not a gold mine."

"That's my best shot. If it doesn't work, then you have to go looking for a marriage counsellor, or a psychologist." Or, she thought, your wife's impecunious lover.

He leaned over the desk and put his hand over hers. "Your best shot is pretty good, and I got value for my money, but you won't mind if I take a rain-check on the advice, will you? I have a feeling it's kind of personal. How much do I owe you?"

The other thing on her mind was her house in Longborough. If Greta's condominium or one like it turned out to be the answer for the future, she would need to sell the Longborough house to raise the down payment.

Her tenant in Longborough still had a month to go on her lease, and had already let Lucy know that she did not intend to ask for a renewal. Lucy was grateful to the house, which had first sheltered her when she ran away from Kingston. It was here that the Trog had appeared one day, in answer to her advertisement offering bed and breakfast, with an offer of his own. He, certainly, was a pleasant ghost, but otherwise she had no sentimental regrets about leaving the house behind. It had served its purpose. The money would do nicely for a down payment on a condominium.

She visited the library to say hello to her old colleagues, their number much reduced by the economies put in place by Longborough's financial managers (though, as her old colleagues pointed out, there were still the same number of people in the financial managers' office), and went home to pack for her trip.

Johnny came in after she had fallen asleep, and he was still asleep at six the next morning when she left to catch her plane.

This time Lucy took a daytime flight. She had flown to England less than a year before, and that was her first flight anywhere in twenty years, and she had been as excited as a child on her first airplane, sitting up all night watching movies and drinking liqueurs. But this time she did not want to spend her first two days in England reorganizing her sleep pattern. A daytime flight seemed the answer.

They landed at Heathrow at eight in the evening and she took the airport bus to the door of her hotel in Bloomsbury. Greta had tried to book her into what she called "a cosy little hotel near Harrods" where Greta stayed on business trips, but Lucy was too recently from Kingston to be able to spend four hundred dollars a night of anybody's money on a bed, so Nina had found her a three-night package in a tourist hotel on Woburn Place for eighty dollars a night. After that, she planned to rent a car and drive down into Cornwall.

She wasted the first day. Having had a good nap on the plane, she was awake, reading, until three o'clock in the morning, London time, sustaining herself on the pack of cheese and crackers that she had kept back from her lunch on the plane. She woke at noon, starving, and ate a large breakfast of scrambled eggs and half-cooked bacon, and went out for a brisk walk.

Everything was both strange and familiar: she roamed around her neighbourhood, taking posession. Russell Square, Bloomsbury, the British Museum, Tottenham Court Road — she was surprised how often she had read these names in detective fiction; she knew them well, although she was unaware of the changes in the streetscape behind these names that had taken place since the golden age of crime, about seventy years before. As far as she was concerned, this was it, the city she knew well, full of wife-murderers, forgers, and bank robbers on the one hand, and pipe-smoking detectives on the other. Even the pubs were as she had expected (she did not see that many of the quainter ones were actually reproductions from the era of her reading; it made no difference). She tried two, and when she saw how small the measures were, had a gin and tonic in each. Many of the customers semed to be American, but there was still a satisfying amount of unintelligible cockney being spoken.

Back in the hotel, she remembered the name of the fish restaurant that Michael Curnow had recommended, and found it was only a few blocks away. She walked there through a light drizzle, just enough to put a gaslight shine on a policeman's cape, if there had been a policeman about with a cape. The recommendation was a good one: she had a fine dinner of superbly fried fish for only twice what it would have cost on Queen Street in Toronto, but the Canadian fish would have been frozen several months before. This was different. She would not have called herself a fish lover, but this was extraordinary, a light golden case of batter enclosing a fillet of plaice so succulent she wanted to grin at the people at the next table. Michael Curnow could be trusted on fish and chips, she realized, and thinking of Curnow, she remembered that she had said she would call him. Perhaps she could pick his brains and give herself a starting point. Perhaps they could meet for a meal or a drink. Ilford couldn't be that far away.

She called early the next morning. Curnow answered his own telephone. "Curnow Investigations," he said, his voice familiar and pleasant to hear. "How can we help you?"

Lucy said, "Michael? Lucy Trimble. Remember me?"

"Lucy. Yes, indeed. As if it was yesterday. Of course it wasn't that long ago, was it, and we've talked on the phone since. How are you?" Then, "This isn't long distance. Are you here? What are you doing here?"

"I'm in Woburn Place, near the British Museum."

He laughed. "Lucy, I *am* glad to hear your voice. So what are you doing near the British Museum?"

"I needed a little break. Greta Golden wanted me to come and take a picture of the place where she was born."

Curnow's voice sharpened. "Why is that? No problem is there? I mean, we sorted that one out, didn't we? Her mother married Aubrey Golden and

had Greta, so Greta's a legitimate heir, as far as that
goes. No question."

Lucy was immediately glad she had replied as she
did. Curnow was not yet to be entirely trusted with
her real mission. "No doubt at all," she said. "But
she'd like some pictures just in case she comes over
herself one day. Sort of like looking up your ancestors. Canadians do it all the time."

"But her ancestors are in Winnipeg."

"Not on her father's side. But that's not what she's
after, anyway. She's just being sentimental about her
birthplace. I mean the building, as well as the town."

"Most people don't care about the building they
were born in, unless it was the family home."

"That's because most people know. It's interesting
to find out if you don't know." She could still feel his
suspicion, but she thought she was handling him well.
"This is just a social call, Michael. I don't know
where Ilford is, but I'll come out there if you like. Get
together for a meal?"

"Get together in Ilford? Whereabouts? No, no. I'll
come up there, where my sister-in-law won't see us.
She sees me helping a lady on to a bus she thinks I'm
getting married again. No, no, there's nowhere to get
together here. Where are you again?"

She told him the name of the hotel.

"I know the place. Across the street there's another hotel with a coffee shop right on the pavement. I'll
meet you there at twelve."

"Could we make it one? It's ten now. I thought I'd
take a quick look at Westminster Abbey."

"Twelve is better. Most people in England eat their
lunch at one, not like Toronto. I noticed the difference

when I was there. We start the day later, finish later, so we're not hungry at twelve. But if you can manage it, it's easier to find a seat at twelve."

"I give in. Twelve it is."

To use the time, Lucy took a tube, going down in the lift at Russell Square and coming up at Knightsbridge. She admired Harrod's for an hour, bought nothing, took a peek at the sumptuous little hotel Greta had wanted her to stay in, without regret, and returned to Bloomsbury a few minutes late to find Curnow sitting in the window of the coffee shop.

"Finding your way, are you? Go anywhere on the tube, can't you?"

"I've figured it all out except the Inner Circle. How does that work?"

"It goes round and round. I was talking to an American the other day who once wanted to go to Knightsbridge, and he asked someone sweeping the platform at Gloucester Road what to do. The sweeper put him on an Inner Circle train and explained how to change on to the Picadilly Line, but he got lost again and got off and asked another sweeper what to do and the bloke said, 'I already told you that an hour ago; now listen to what I'm saying,' and put him back on the Inner Circle train." Curnow laughed. "Now," he said. "What's all this, then?"

She smiled dutifully. "I told you. Greta wants me to find out where she was born. The actual building."

"That's a load of tommy rot," he said, but smiling to take away any offence. "There's something fishy about the circumstances surrounding the birth of your client, isn't there?"

"Not that we know of." Lucy felt confident of being able to hold her own with Curnow in the short term.

"Don't try to kid me, Lucy, old girl. But I've been thinking. I've got a proposition. Why don't we team up?"

"How? What for?"

"I gave my client a ring after you phoned me ..."

She interrupted him. "Michael, I know who your clients are. The relatives, right? Tucker and Tucker are not the people handling the will."

"You've deduced that, have you? Well done. Yes. I told them you had to be here for a reason, so I've been instructed to find out what you are up to. That's why we're having lunch, on me. I don't normally come up to London if I can avoid it. I hate the place. By the way, why *did* you ring me up?"

"Just social," she said. "I don't know anyone else in England."

"Lucy Trimble," he said. "That's English. Don't you have ancestors here?"

"Lieutenant Trimble was an officer in the army during the War of Independence. He was a Loyalist, and came over after the war to homestead in Ontario, or Upper Canada as it was then."

"I stand amazed. You people have more history than I thought. So shall we team up?"

"You can give me a start. Point me in the right direction."

"See? I knew it wasn't my looks." He showed his teeth. "What sort of start?"

"I know where she was born."

"Shale. Right?"

"You've done your homework."

"I've seen the birth certificate."

"I thought you might be able to tell me what the normal procedures were here, in the country, thirty-eight years ago. Would it have been a hospital? A maternity hospital? A nursing home? Or what?"

"The address of the nursing home — the most likely place to have a baby, back then — would be on the certificate. No, wait a minute. That would be the parents' Canadian address. Aubrey Golden, book-keeper, and June Golden, spouse. We'll have to start from scratch."

"We? I haven't agreed yet."

"Look. My client wants to know what you're up to. To find that out, they'll pay me a per diem and all expenses, within reason. Say four days. *Your* client will do the same, yes? Now you and I know I won't find out anything interesting, though I have a feeling that you're up to something you're not telling about. And I think I know what it is. *You* think you'll find out who the real father is, starting at this end, don't you? After forty years. Not a hope, Lucy, my old girl. Forty years ago someone diddled Greta's mother and did a bunk, probably out to Saskatoon. Greta's mother thereupon conned Aubrey Golden into marrying her because in those days they were still declaring children illegitimate on the birth certificate. So Aubrey did his job, and then fell off a cliff the next day. Were they very close?"

Lucy said, "I'm trying to think. Greta said they were, but she got that from her mother, of course. The only other person who was around then was Jim McSweeney."

"Who?"

Lucy explained. "The point is that Jim McSweeney would say that, wouldn't he? He'd be part of the cover-up."

"What the hell are you talking about?"

"Suppose it wasn't an accident. Suppose Aubrey Golden was murdered."

"God Almighty, there you go. Why, for Heaven's sake?"

"I don't know. Yet."

Curnow started to laugh. "It's a thought, though, isn't it? Make a nice legal point, I would think. If *she* killed him, and he wasn't Greta's father, then should Greta be allowed to profit by her mother's criminal act? I mean if the intention in marrying him was to provide the baby with a name, and she killed him as soon as the kid was born, then that might mean neither she nor the baby should profit. Know what I mean?"

"You're not serious."

"I wasn't, but now there's *doubt*. Lawyers love doubt. Given a half-decent doubt a half-decent lawyer could tie up this claim for years if my client felt vindictive and didn't mind spending the whole bundle on lawyer's fees. Contests over wills are meat and drink to those buggers. Meat and drink."

"And to you."

"What? Well, yes, there's that." He grinned lopsidely. "But I might come back with something to show for my client's money, mightn't I? So where do we start?"

"With how people in England were born in 1957."

"I was only a nipper then, myself. I'll give my auntie a ring. She's in her seventies now. She'll know."

"Is that what private detectives do here? Give auntie a ring?"

"Now, now. You won't get a rise out of me on that. I'm the real thing, not some shoot-em-up dick in a novel. In this case my auntie is the best starting point. Now, how did you plan to go down to Cornwall?"

"I'm renting a car."

He looked thoughtfully out at Woburn Place. "Have you ever driven here?"

"No, but it can't be that difficult. I was frightened of Toronto traffic once."

"Did you plan to drive in London? This isn't Toronto. I know a lot of English people who won't drive in London. You know you'll be on the wrong side of the road?"

"Don't pat me on the head. Everyone knows that."

"No. Lucy, everyone has heard it, but you have to get behind the wheel to really know it. Did you order an automatic? No? Then you'll get a standard. Standard is still ... standard over here. Can you drive with a gear shift? Come with me. Let me do the driving."

"No. I haven't agreed to team up yet. Anyway, I want to drive. But I can't drive standard."

"Then list me as a second driver and we'll go down together in your automatic."

"No."

"Why not?"

"Because I don't want you following me around."

"You *are* up to something."

"I'm not looking for whoever killed Greta's father. I just made that up. I merely want to go around by myself. You can investigate the death of Greta's father, if you like, and good luck to you. I'm just going to find out where she was born and take some pictures. Okay?"

He looked at her with a finger laid against his nose, smiling a half-finished smile. "I'll stay out of your way. It'll be a lot easier for you with me as chauffeur. I'll pick you up in the morning, and we'll go on from here. We'll leave my car at the garage when we pick up yours. We'll spend a few minutes getting you familiar with the traffic over this side, the left-hand driving."

It was a point that had begun to trouble her. She was a perfectly competent driver, she told herself (although she still tried to avoid the 401 highway in the rush hour with its sometimes sixteen lanes of traffic), and she was determined never again to be intimidated by any driving situation which the natives regarded as normal, wherever she found herself. Greta, she was sure, raced around England without a second thought; all Lucy had to do was close her eyes, metaphorically, and dive in. But there was no need to be foolish. It might be useful to have someone watch her for a few minutes. "All right." She dug in her shoulder bag for the wallet that contained all her documents. "I was supposed to pick the car up at nine o'clock at somewhere called Holland Park."

"Phone them. Make sure they have an automatic for you. I'll be outside at half-past eight." He pointed out to the street. "Wait at the curb. Now. What are you going to do with yourself this afternoon?"

"Walk."

"Where?"

"Wherever. I've been looking at my map. I think I could walk from here to Picadilly Circus and back. If not, I'll get a cab home from wherever I find myself."

"Don't you want to see Buckingham Palace? Big Ben. St Paul's. Things like that?"

"I know what all those look like. I'll do a tour one day, but this afternoon I want to be on my feet, mixing with the natives, getting a feel of the place."

"Walking."

"Yes."

He sighed. "I *was* going to offer to drive you round, point out the sights. I know Central London like the back of my hand. I'm not going on a walking tour, though."

"I'll go on my own, then."

"Couple of things. Do me a favour, leave your handbag at the hotel."

"My purse?"

"Whatever you call the thing you keep your money in. Take a few quid stuffed up your jumper."

"How much?"

"Twenty pounds. For fares and a cup of tea. Then it won't matter if you walk along with a map in your hand, mispronouncing the names like the rest of them."

"I don't plan to do that. I thought I'd make a list of the places along the way, after I've looked at the map, and ask my way from one to the next, like someone up from Ilford for the day."

He laughed. "No one will mistake you for someone from Ilford with that accent. Still, it might be a good idea. Just go up to someone and ask them how to get to so and so, you mean? And then do the same for the next bit? That might work. Keep it simple, though. Let's have a look at that map. All right, write this down. Got a bit of paper? Use my newspaper. Now, start off on this road outside. Walk down to

Holborn Station. Have a look at the old houses on Holborn, if they're still there. Next, ask for the Strand. Walk along the Strand until you see a sign for Covent Garden. All right? Have a look round Covent Garden, then, when you get lost, ask for Leicester Square. From there, anyone will direct you to Picadilly Circus."

"Where's Soho?"

"Why?"

"I've heard of it."

"What have you heard?"

"It's sleazy, isn't it? Full of tarts and pimps and sex shops? I thought I might take a look."

"Got some nice restaurants, too, I think. It's years since I was in Soho. I used to know it like ..."

"Did you have your first experience in Soho, like the heroes in those growing-up-in-London novels?" She used a tone to show that her question was intended to be more jocular than personal, just light-hearted banter, but she was curious.

"I was in a diferent novel. I lost mine on the beach at Clacton, actually, underneath the pier. But, yes, I didn't see anything like Soho in Toronto. Have a look, then, on your way back. You'll be all right. You don't look like a tart. Or a madam."

"What do I look like?"

"A tourist from Canada. Never mind. I expect I stick out like a sore thumb in Toronto."

"Only when you speak. Where do I go on to from Soho?"

"St. Giles Circus. Then the British Museum. Then Russell Square. Then home. You know the name of your hotel? Good. Don't forget, Woburn Place. You sure you don't want company? I could manage the walking if you insist."

"No. Once more. First, going: Holborn, the Strand, Covent Garden, Leicester Square, Picadilly Circus. Coming back: Soho, St. Giles, the British Museum, Russell Square, Woburn Square."

"You'll be all right."

"Before I go, though, I need something for my eyes. I think I'm starting a cold."

"Gritty, are they?"

"Yes, I need to find a drugstore."

"A chemist's shop is what you want. It's just filth. Pollution. Look up there: completely clear sky, except for the haze. That's made of diesel and petrol fumes, and it's full of rubbish that gets in your eyes. The modern equivalent of the good old London fog."

"Toronto is polluted, too, but this seems pretty harsh. Maybe it affects foreigners more, like the water in Mexico. Maybe you get used to it."

"If I could, I'd move into the country, but there's not much call for security services in Lower Sodbury. We're doomed, Lucy, so let's have a couple of days in Cornwall, while we can still breathe."

She spent a lot of time in an agreeable maze of streets behind the opera house, and drank a cup of coffee in the piazza while a trio of students played a bit of Haydn, impressing Lucy that such arcane music could be offered in a public square. She put a pound in the cloth bag that was handed round the crowd and plunged back into the maze. She was soon lost and asking for directions to Leicester Square, and then decided on what seemed like a shortcut and found herself in Soho.

She spent a pleasant half hour in a giant fruit and vegetable market, wondering where the action was, and then she took a good look down a side street and saw the signs advertising SEX.

She had never seen a pornographic image, either still or moving, that she could remember, and she was sure that one day she would be confronted with some in the course of her work. She knew the terms but she did not know the difference between soft-core and hard-core, and what she would have liked would be to go in to one of these shops and buy two soft-core and two hard-core magazines, ask for a chair, read them, then give them back for the owner to sell to someone in need. That way she could avoid finding herself in hospital with a bag full of pornography (having been knocked down by a taxi on her way back to the hotel), trying to explain to the nurses that it was just research. She needed Nina with her, or, better, Peter Tse, who claimed to have grown up in Soho, although now that she'd seen it she found it difficult to imagine a family life being lived in a street market lined with cafés and film companies.

She strolled down the street, window-shopping, but there was nothing in the windows that wasn't on display at her local bread-and-milk store in Toronto. She saw that she would have to pass through one of those beaded-curtain doorways to get a real eye-opener, but the street came to an end before she could bring herself to do it, and then there was nothing except Chinese restaurants. She walked back on the other side, testing herself and failing, and she was

once more in the street market, where she bought
some apples for her journey down to Cornwall and a
banana to eat on the spot.

And then she was tired, and she walked steadily in
the same direction until she found herself in Charing
Cross Road from where she was easily directed to St.
Giles, and the museum and home. Across from the
hotel, she found a pub, and drank a gin-and-tonic and
got winked at in an entirely collegial way by one of the
regulars who took her for a local, and decided that next
time she needed three days on her feet in London.

Chapter Sixteen

Curnow pulled into the curb, leaned over to open the passenger door, took Lucy's overnight bag off her, threw it behind him, took her arm to help her into the car, leaned across her to close the door, all in one linked motion but not quickly enough to retain the hole in the traffic he had left, and they had to wait several minutes before a kindly taxi-driver, or one who needed their spot, let them into the traffic surging towards Holborn, a flood of trucks, Rolls Royces — lots of these — minis, cyclists, delivery vans, cars with three wheels, all of whom seemed to know exactly how to navigate the white arrows painted on the road, and the lights directing the different lanes, and how to part the sea of pedestrians that filled the intersections when the lights changed, part them without damaging any.

Curnow was good, seeming quite comfortable in this jostling tide of vehicles, picking his way through without being assaulted or spat on for cutting in, a necessary manoeuvre because of the many sudden changes of direction, and they emerged from the rapids of Marble Arch into the calm fast waters of the Bayswater Road and raced westward to the Holland Park garage.

"I need a cup of coffee," Lucy said. She was badly shaken, now that she had seen London traffic.

"Get signed up, and don't forget to include me as a second driver. Then wait in the office. I'll arrange for them to keep my car until we get back."

While she was signing rental papers, Curnow picked up two paper cups of coffee and they sat in the office while he went over the map of the local streets with her. "We'll go for a little spin on the back streets until you get used to the left-hand drive. Once we are on the road, it's a straight run."

When she was ready, the clerk led them to her car, got Lucy seated and leaned through the window. "Turn signals, lights, flasher, hooter, cigarette lighter, radio, windscreen wiper, petrol release, bonnet release, window up-and-down, pedals on the floor, here's a map, bring it back full up." And left.

"See?" Curnow said. "You don't know which way is up, do you? Let's give it a try."

For a quarter of an hour he took her patiently through the rudiments of operating the car and steering it through the West London traffic. "You know how roundabouts work?" He asked. "I never saw one in Toronto."

"No."

He took a notebook from his pocket and drew a little diagram, explaining as he went. "Now let's try one. Straight ahead, turn left, here we go. Yes,

hang on, no, stay in the lane, never mind the honking, now we'll have to go round again. Put your
signal on, now exit left. NOW! Good girl. Let's do
it once more."

They did it twice more, and Lucy said, "If we're
going to Cornwall today, we'd better make a start."

"Right. Go left here, now left again. There. Pull
up behind the green car."

Curnow got out and came round to her side of
the car, waiting for her to get out and change places.
Lucy stayed where she was, her hands still gripping
the wheel, a trickle of perspiration running down
between her breasts. "I'll drive," she said.

"Once we get out of London."

"Now. If I'm going to do it, now's the time to
start, with you here. It couldn't be a better situation."

"You're not joking?"

She shook her head and started the engine.

"Right, then. If anything happens to me, and you
survive, you'll find my sister's address in my wallet.
Off we go, then. No, wait for a gap, then off we go.
Trot on, then, in your own time. You are watching for
signs to the M4, all right?"

It wasn't a piece of cake, but after the first couple
of miles it seemed possible that one day she would be
able to do this alone. Once more, Curnow was splen-
did, talking continually at first, describing the road
ahead, and the traffic, feeding her warnings about
possible developments ahead, guiding her round the
larger roundabouts, then shutting up where he felt she
could get on with it. London went on for a long time,
but eventually they passed Heathrow and Lucy felt
properly on her way westward.

She tried to stay in the second lane as she did on the 401, but a lot of honking and light-flashing moved her over to the curb lane, where she stayed, overtaking only when it slowed too much even for her, once, incredibly, for a tiny Austin made in about 1920 with what looked like solid tires and containing two ladies, the driver with a hat tied on with a scarf, and a very old lady holding onto her hat, travelling at about fifteen miles an hour.

Curnow pointed comically to his mouth and she looked at her watch, amazed to see that it was twelve-thirty, and nodded and drove into an eating place attached to a service station.

She explained to the boy behind the counter that she wanted a bacon, tomato and lettuce sandwich, pointing to the piece of bacon she wanted. "Streaky?" he asked, in disbelief. "Got a nice rasher here." He held up a piece of bacon the size and colour of a gorilla's palm, with the rind still on it.

"Streaky," she said. "And crisp."

"Right," he said in disgust. "How about this? Shrivelled enough for you? Salad cream is on the table."

The tea was superb — strong, fresh and gutsy. "With tea like this you don't miss coffee," Lucy said.

Curnow, in front of a plate of eggs, bacon, sausages, baked beans, tomatoes and fried bread, over which he had trailed a garnishing thread of HP sauce, said, "It's nice being on expenses. Usually I take a sandwich to work. Cheese and pickle, or egg and tomato. This is a treat. Now," he opened a map and flattened it out between them. "We're here. Reading. We go straight out past Bath to the M5, then down to Exeter, where we pick up the A30 to Launceston. Then we go across country to Shale. I thought we might stay here overnight." He pointed to a name on the coast. "It's been recommended. I'll phone ahead. Without a booking we might find accomodation a bit tight this time of the year."

"Should you call now?"

"I'll do it from Launceston, or p'raps Exeter. Yes. Three hours with a bit of luck. We should have enough petrol if we fill up now."

The motorway was like all motorways, entirely unrelated to the surrounding countryside. Lucy recognized the names of towns that she had come across in her reading, Newbury (Dick Francis), Bath (Jane Austen), Taunton (Lorna Doone). But the motorway did not seem to be part of the world these signs represented.

By the time they reached Chippenham the driving had become easy and slightly boring. Curnow said, "You maried, Lucy?"

"I was once."

"What happened?"

"I left him."

"Why?"

"He was a control freak."

"Ah."

That was as far as she wanted the conversation to go in that direction. "And you?" she asked. "You're a widower?"

"Yes."

"With a ten-year-old daughter."

"Pamela."

"And a sister."

"And, since you are counting, three sisters."

"Do you get along with them all?"

"Very well. They look after Pamela any time I have to go away, and she likes staying with all of them."

"Sounds like someone I know in Toronto. What do you do with yourself? Apart from ..."

"I'm a gardener. That's another reason I'd like to live in the country, apart from getting away from the smog. I'd like a big garden. Then I would have it all."

"A real Englishman. Nothing missing?"

"If you mean, do I want to get married again, I don't think so. The risk for Pamela is too big, and the longer I live alone, with her, the more I like it."

Her question had been unspecific, but his reply assumed she was fishing.

She looked out at the passing countryside. "At home the trees are starting to turn. It still looks like summer here."

He accepted the change of subject. "We've had a good one," he said. "After a wet spring."

Then at Exeter they stopped for tea and a slice of fruit cake, and Curnow did some telephoning. He came back with the news that the inn at Rockingham Cove had a double bed and a single. "I told them to put me down for the double and you the single," he said. "We can do a swap when we get there."

"Why?"

"Double costs twice as much, so I'll put it on my expenses and we could split the total between us. See, I need a bill. I don't think you do, but if you do, we'll get them to make copies of both bills and we can explain to our respective clients that they got the bills muddled up, but each of us can say we had the double."

Lucy worked her way through this. "Is there much money involved?"

"The double, with breakfast, is seventy pounds. The single is forty. Total a hundred and ten. Now if we both put in for the double we'll be fifteen quid each in pocket." He stood up. "Now, over the moor to Launceston, and then across to Rockingham Cove. Not more than a couple of hours I wouldn't think. There's plenty of light left yet."

"But it's no distance at all compared to what we've done. Why will it take so long?"

"You'll see."

Lucy felt the force of his warning immediately, as they left the protection of the motorway for the bustle of the real world with houses, trees, side streets, roundabouts, cyclists and a horse-drawn trap. On the other hand she was glad finally to see England.

"Where's Dartmoor?" she asked.

"Behind us."

"We've missed it?"

"I didn't know it was on your itinerary."

"Of course it is. I want to see the prison. We'll have to look on the way back. Do they still fire a gun when a prisoner escapes?"

"You're thinking of the hulks. The prison ships. A hundred years ago. Actually they don't even lock the prisoners up anymore. It's not a maximum security prison."

"I'd still like to see it."

They bypassed Launceston and turned onto a narrower road, no more than a lane with passing places carved out of the verge at intervals.

"What's that?" Lucy said, jamming on her brakes.

"It's a grid. You must have heard of them. They are to prevent sheep from escaping."

"Can I drive over it?"

"That's what it's for."

They drove up a rise in the road and came to a small lay-by that commanded a modest view of the moor.

"Stop for a minute," Curnow said.

She turned off the engine and they looked at the world in front of them.

"Those are the sheep," he said pointing, "and look, those are wild ponies."

"You mean no one owns them? And what are those metal things? They look like space creatures."

"Those are windmills. You are looking at a wind farm. A lot of people object to the sight of them. They feel they pollute the landscape."

Lucy considered. "I like them," she said finally. "And now here comes the famous mist, which the prisoners use to escape by. We'd better get going."

But it was only a patch and they drove through it and to the top of the next hill and Lucy said, "What's that?"

"What?" He peered round, alarmed.

"The sea! We've reached the sea!"

They came down finally through the straggle of houses that made up the village of Rockingham Cove, down to the sea where they turned and parked in the lot above the pub. "Made it," she said. "One little curb on a roundabout, that's all we hit."

She got out of the car, her knees stiff and her back slightly achy, but feeling qualified by her day's experience to drive herself to wherever the truth was to be found.

The inn stood alone on the seafront except for a small café on the other side of the little square. It was not an old building, but it seemed to have been carefully fitted into the cliff wall. On the ground floor, an ice-cream parlour opened out on to the square, and the public rooms, the two bars and the restaurant took up the first floor overlooking the sea. The bedrooms were one floor higher.

They found a door open at the back of the building and walked into a small lobby. When they rang the little bell on the counter of the registration desk, the door to the bar opened and a barman said, "Looking for a room? We're all full up."

"We have a reservation," Curnow said.

The barman said, "Curnow? Mr. Curnow?"

"That's right."

The barman said, "You're expected," and took two keys off the wall and handed them to Curnow. "You can sign the book later," he said. "The stairs are behind you."

"We'll have a wash and brush up," Curnow said to Lucy. "I'll meet you here in half an hour." He pointed through the door. "Over by the window. We'd better have dinner here, save getting back on the road again. Better warn the kitchen." He led them through to the bar.

A portion of the room was furnished with dining tables, and there was a sign on the portable chalkboard, "Fresh Cod." "Hullo," Curnow said. "We're in luck. Any cod left?" he asked the barman.

"I'll find out." The barman disappeared and returned almost immediately. "Just a couple of portions left. She's saving them for you. All right?" He took a damp cloth and wiped the chalk board clean. Then he wrote, "Bar Food," and turned back to them.

"I'm presuming, aren't I?" Curnow said. "You *do* like fish?"

"What's so special about cod?"

"*Fresh*," Curnow said. "Caught today, that means, place like this." He pointed out the window to the sea. "Out there."

He picked up the leather-cased bar menu, "Everything else is frozen. Right?"

"'Cept the sausages," the barman agreed.

Curnow moved Lucy towards the door. "Half an hour, then," he said, and gave her the key to the single room.

Sitting in the window of the bar, looking out at the sea, a half-pint of best bitter in front of her, Lucy felt herself in luck. From her seat she could look down on the little cove which had once, she was sure, been used by smugglers dodging revenue men, though there were no boats of any kind there now. The sea gathered itself in the distance under the early evening sun and raced towards the cove, throwing itself on the beach, or shore, or strand — whatever — with a satisfying roar followed by the sucking sound of the shingles as the waves regathered for the next run, endlessly .... Lucy promised herself to buy some Daphne du Maurier when she could find a bookstore.

The cod had been delicious, every bit as tasty as her last dinner in the fish bar near her hotel. Afterwards she had had a taste of Curnow's sticky toffee pudding, but managed to say no for herself, and refused coffee in favour of another half-pint of beer, which she hoped would put her to sleep.

Curnow said, "Fancy a toddle along the cliffs?"

"Is it safe at night?"

"Plenty of light about yet. I don't think there are many pirates left." Curnow grinned.

The cliff path began almost outside their window, across the road which ran past the hotel, and followed the coastline south. They walked along, keeping carefully to the footpath. Lucy had packed her running shoes, intending them to serve as bedroom slippers if the bathroom was down the hall, and now she was glad because the path worn into the cliff was full of small boulders and pockets in the chalk, problems for any kind of heels. Sometimes it sloped from back to front, so that it was easier to walk above it, along the tussocky ground. She was glad, too, when they came to the first of several stiles, that she was wearing trousers, because she was one of those people who, halfway across a stile find they have put the wrong foot down and are now facing backwards, groping for the step. The gusty wind, exhilarating as she found it, would have blown her skirts about her head.

"You independent now Lucy, Fancy free?"

Here it comes, Lucy thought. "Look, look at those birds. What are they? Swallows?"

"Sand martins I think. Are you?"

"What? Oh, no. I live with a ... man in Toronto."

"Oh, yes. What does he do, then?"

"He trains racehorses."

"Does he really? Known him long?"

"Long enough to move in with him, and don't ask how long that is. What about you? When did your wife die?"

"Three years ago." Curnow paused, waiting for another question. When it didn't come, he went on, anyway. "I haven't been with anyone else since. It would have felt as if I was being unfaithful, which I never was." He found something to look at out to sea.

This, thought Lucy, is the stranger-on-holiday chat, when you can tell him or her everything because you'll never see one another again. Some writers of mysteries used it as a revelation scene, to return to when the speaker was found washed up on the rocks. Even though Lucy had had little enough experience, she knew that in life, too, confessing personal matters of a non-criminal nature to strangers abroad was not uncommon. But Curnow had to be cut off before he went too far. All the time they talked, they had been scrambling along the cliff walk, which now seemed to Lucy to have come hair-raisingly, casually, close to the edge. A very long way below them the surf pounded on, waiting to smash any humans it caught on the rocks along the shore. Lucy said, "You sound like a good husband. Let's take the other path higher up and go back. I think I can sleep now." And then, inevitably, she stumbled and he caught her around the waist.

And that was all there was to it. Once they had found solid ground, he removed his arm, and, relieved, she linked her arm in his for the walk back to the inn. In five minutes they would be back at the inn. "There's the moon," she said and quickened their steps up the path to the main road.

In front of the hotel, he said, "A night-cap?"

She shook her head. "I'm going to bed." Curnow smiled. "Sleep well," he said, and opened the door for her.

It was much later, thinking about it all in Cambridge, that she came to the embarrassed realization that far from planning, in Greta's phrase, to get a leg over, for most of the trip Curnow had been just as careful as she not to respond to what seemed to him like overtures from her.

At breakfast they sat at the same table by the window. Curnow had not arrived when Lucy came down, but as she was seated he came in from the outside door. His demeanour was cheerful and he smiled so warmly that she thought he might ask for a kiss.

"Morning," he said, flapping a napkin, and rubbing his hands. "Lovely morning. Went for a little stroll the other way." He pointed through the window to the much higher cliff on the other side of the cove. Two couples were climbing the cliff path in the distance, one couple getting smaller as they toiled about halfway up, the other, near the top, were tiny, ant-like.

"There's no guard rail, at all," Lucy said, to herself as much as to him.

"It's safe enough, if you aren't drunk."

"It would be easy to push someone off, though, wouldn't it?"

"You'd have to persuade them to come up there with you in the first place, wouldn't you? I mean ... oh, Lucy, you're at it again. Now you've seen it, we're back with murder, right? Well, have your fun. But remember, they haven't been sitting around here for forty years waiting for you to come along and tell them what really happened. They would have thought of that and checked up on it."

"All I said was ..." She let it go.

"What's the drill now?" he asked, as he demolished a large fried breakfast. "I like a place that gives you mushrooms," he added.

"I don't know what you're going to do. I'm going in to Shale to take some pictures."

"Want some company?"

"Not really. What do your clients think you're doing?"

"Keeping an eye on you, and investigating the circumstances of Aubrey Golden's death. Like I said."

"Then why don't you do that? You find out who killed Aubrey, and I'll find out where Greta was born."

"Making fun, are we? That's all right, I don't mind. You know, it's very nice being here, on a day like this, with you." He pushed himself back from the table sharply, and stood up.

"Where to now?" she asked.

"You just said it. Find out who killed Aubrey Golden. How long do you need in Shale? I'll take you in, then follow the trail to Golden's killer. Couple of hours? We could be back for lunch."

"Fine. I'll drive."

Chapter Seventeen

The road to Shale was two lanes wide; after the single lanes around Rockingham Cove, it seemed spacious. The actual driving was no longer a problem: she had learned to watch for road signs wherever they were to be found — on posts, on the sides of buildings, painted on the road; roundabouts were now a breeze, though the tiny double roundabouts that were no more than two rings of white paint like a giant optician's advertisement, painted usually where three roads joined — these were beyond her. At these she simply stopped until the honking grew obsessive and obviously directed at her before she proceeded, or if there were no hedges, and she was certain there was no other traffic, drove straight across them.

The fact that one set of signposts with place-names would be replaced within a mile or two by an entirely different set of names in different colours, making it seem like a different road she had wandered onto in her sleep, was no longer a problem. The old names and the old colours soon returned, she had found. So it was possible to drive, but not yet to drive automatically or with any instinct and still leave room in the brain for other kinds of thought. Every manoeuvre required to be anticipated and mentally rehearsed if she did not want to get herself stuck in the lane which turned into the queue for the multi-storeyed car park, a single-laned queue with a brick wall on one side and a barricade on the other. You had to know, a quarter of a mile away, not to get into that lane. She passed a tractor pulling a flat-bed after the boy driving the tractor had stood up to signal that the road was clear, and gave the boy a wave. Piece of cake. On the edge of Shale she saw a sign directing her to a car park so she parked and they walked into the centre of Shale where Curnow left her, arranging to meet back at that spot in two hours. Lucy found a policeman, and got the direction she sought. She had the address written on a piece of paper.

"Can you tell me where thirty-two Lock Street is located?" she said, clear as a bell.

The policeman held out his hand for the piece of paper.

"Thirty-two Lock Street," Lucy repeated, crunching the consonants and intoning the vowels as if she were programming a voice-activated computer.

He smiled and held out his hand for the piece of paper. When he got it, he smiled again and settled himself down to translate. "You want thirty-two Lock Street," he said.

Lucy wondered how people from Alabama got on in Shale.

The policeman took her arm, twisted her through a hundred and eighty degrees and pointed down the road that ran off the square. "Go deuwn to the Barley Mow, take the roight-hand lane and keep on to the bo'om. That's Lock Street. You can't miss it. No, no. Don't turn reund, you'll get lost. Foller yer nose straight deuwn to' the bo'om. All roight?"

"Thanks a lot."

"Beg your pardon?"

"Thanks. Thank you."

"Ah. Don't forget. Don't look left or roight 'til you're at the Barley Mow."

She did as she was told and fifteen minutes later she was standing outside number thirty-two as promised. On the door, in gold lettering, was a sign, "The Shale Vein Clinic. Walk in."

Behind a counter, a woman in a green smock was cursing the display screen of a computer and talking on the telephone. "Come on," she said. "Come on, come on. Christ! Yes?" The last word was addressed to Lucy.

"I'm looking for a maternity home," Lucy said.

"You'll be out by two o'clock. Make sure you have someone to pick you up. You have to be escorted home. You what?" this last to Lucy. She returned to the telephone. "No, this is a private clinic. Fee-paying, yes. Yes, an examination is required. Tomorrow if you like. The National Health takes a year. Right. Call us when you're ready." She swung back to Lucy. "Yes? Oh, right. The maternity home. Not for you, I hope. Sorry, what do they call that — ageist, that's it. You could be carrying twins, couldn't you? But the maternity home went years ago. Sorry? Yes? Vein Clinic. Just a minute. He's in surgery now. Pick him up at two o'clock. Be a bit groggy, but he'll be able to walk. If he could before."

Lucy turned away and nearly fell over a woman who was mopping the hall. "Wha'ever do you want the maternity 'ome for? I'm about the only one left who remembers them. Twenty years it must've been. I used to char for them." She looked up at Lucy sideways, not bothering to straighten up.

"Where would the records be stored? I'm trying to find the record of someone who was born in 1957."

"I wasn't 'ere *then*, was I? I'm not that old. I may bleeding look it, but I'm not. I've just had a hard life. I'm sixty-five, but I know I look older. When I was fifty I looked sixty-five, so would anyone who'd put up with what I put up with."

"Town Hall. Births and Deaths," the woman behind the counter called.

"Where's that?"

But the telephone claimed her again. The cleaner said, "What do you want to know, then?" She pulled herself upright.

"I was hoping I would find someone who was working here at that time."

"Long while ago, 'n it?"

"Forty years."

"It's been a vein clinic for ten years, ever since people had to wait so long for the National 'Ealth lot."

"It's a private clinic?" Lucy swivelled her eyes to include the woman behind the counter who was listening to them with her head averted.

"Bleeding gold mine, that's what this is," the charwoman said. "It's private, all right. Wait a minute, wait a minute. I know 'oo you want. When this place closed up as a maternity 'ome, there was one midwife who they said'd been 'ere from the start. I don't know about

that, but she 'ad been here all 'er life. Old Nan. Short
for Nanny. Still alive, still got all 'er marbles. I see 'er
in Budgen's sometimes, on a Friday night. Deaf as a
post but always seems to catch the important things,
the things she wants to 'ear. One of those. Sharp as a
tack, she is. Good old soul, though. Learned to drive
when she was sixty-five, she did. Gave it up when she
got too deaf to 'ear all the 'ooters." She whooped lightly, joyfully at the memory of old Nan driving deafly
through the town, pantomiming her holding the steering wheel. "I'll tell you where she lives. Find Berring's
Lane. I won't try to direct you because it's too 'ard for
a stranger. Go out of 'ere, turn right, and when you
come to the first corner, ask someone to point the way
to the War Memorial. When you get there, ask again.
Now when you get to Berring's Lane, you'll find a little row of cottages on the right 'and side, three of
them, built together for farm labourers, I should think.
You know, two up, two down, and the lavatory at the
end of the garden. Now. Mind. Nanny owns all three.
She brought them for ha'pence, donkey's years ago,
and 'ad them done up over the years — 'ot water, double glazing, all that. She lives in the first one and lets
the other two out, mainly to 'oliday-makers. So what
with 'er gratuity when she left 'ere, and the pension,
and what she saved, though give 'er credit she was
always openhanded, still she must be worth a tidy
penny, but bloody good luck to 'er." She ended aggres-
sively, shouting. "She did it all by herself. I wish I'd
been on my own. Marriage is a bloody indignity, that's
all it is. Nothing in it for a woman. You married? Anyway, you'll need every penny if you want yer veins
done 'ere."

Lucy perceived that the charwoman was so deeply aggrieved by her condition as to be nearly maddened by it. "I was married once," she said, moving away.

"'Ere," the woman said, grabbing her arm and pulling her close. "What did yer do with 'im? Eh?" She giggled. "Arsenic?"

Lucy slid away and out on to the street. As she left she heard behind her the charwoman shouting at the receptionist. "You 'ear what I said to 'er?" she demanded from across the hall. "I asked 'er if she give 'er husband arsenic."

"Mrs. Barfield?"

Nanny stood in the wide-open doorway, one hand on the doorframe, the other on the door. She was small, and probably slightly shrunken from her natural height, but erect, without any of the stoop and shuffle a working woman of eighty was entitled to. Her hair was dark grey but still thick, parted on the side and held back by a single large tortoiseshell clip. She was wearing a flowered apron that crossed over in the front and tied behind her back, and a pair of old black shoes as slippers.

"Who wants to know?" she demanded, not unpleasantly, but by way of taking the initiative. "Speak up. I'm deaf." Lucy could imagine her holding the newborn infant high, slapping its bottom, tying the thread around the umbilical cord and handing the child to a waiting relative, checking the time of the birth by a watch which hung on a leather strap from a button hole. A woman in charge.

"My name is Lucy Trimble. I'm from Canada on a visit and doing a little research on a friend's family history, a friend in Toronto," she shouted.

"You don't know my nephew, I suppose? Jacob Barfield. He went out there thirty years ago. Haven't heard anything since." She burst into giggles. "Don't look so worried. I'm just teasing you. It's what people say, isn't it? 'You live in London? My sister lives in London. P'raps you know her.' Come in, then, see if I can help."

The front door led directly into the parlour, a small space with a polished linoleum floor, and furnished with an armchair on either side of the fireplace, a small spindle-backed settee facing the fire, and a drop-leaf dining table and four Windsor chairs against the wall by the kitchen door. The rest of the room was filled with low tables, small ones by the armchairs and at each end of the settee, and several larger ones which held projects in different stages of completion — a jigsaw puzzle, a piece of embroidery — and a knitting bag.

"No, no, don't follow me about. You sit there while I put the kettle on. I haven't tidied up yet. Here, read the paper." She sat Lucy in one of the armchairs and threw a newspaper at her, a tabloid with a headline occupying the whole page, "Queen For a Day, p. 3." The headline on page three said, "Lorry Driver Achieves Life's Ambition," over a picture of a truck driver in a wedding dress. Lucy began to read, but Nanny returned with a tea tray and whisked the paper out of her hand. "Load of rubbish," she said. "But it burns better than the *Telegraph*." She nodded towards the carefully laid fire, awaiting the next cold snap. "You get it all on the telly, anyway. Now, what can I do for you?"

Lucy took a sip of tea. "A friend of mine was born here," she began.

"Speak up. How old is this friend? Your age. You'd be about fifty, I'd say," she said appraisingly.

"I *am* fifty. My friend is forty."

"I can see this leading up to the day she was born at Valleyfield, so I wondered. I was working there forty years ago, not fifty."

"Did you deliver all the babies in 1957?"

"Not all of them. They had a resident doctor. Dead now, he is. No, I delivered all the babies I had charge of, although the matron would sometimes call in the doctor over my head. Don't misunderstand me. I called the doctor in myself if I got into a complication, even if I thought I could manage. But she sometimes did it unnecessarily. The doctor was all right, just a nuisance sometimes. But you don't want to hear all this. Let me tell you how it worked, so you'll know. If a mother decided to have her baby at home, naturally, like, then she might have a doctor or she might have me. In those days there wasn't a lot of the fuss you get now in these prenatal clinics. I used to visit once a month — I'm a qualified nurse *and* a midwife — then later on, once a week. In the last few days I might move in to the spare room and stay for a day or two until after they were well set. You don't have midwives in Canada, do you." It wasn't a question.

"In some provinces we do."

Nanny shook her head, firmly. "No. You ask someone when you get back. You'll find they're not allowed. They should be, but they're not. The point

I'm making is that if there was any real trouble coming up, a very protracted labour, for example, then I got an ambulance and transferred my patient to Valleyfield where I had privileges."

Lucy decided that her main objective wouldn't be furthered by getting into an argument. "Privileges?" she asked.

"I could deliver in the maternity home as long as the mother requested, though the doctor had to have a look at her. Now, who were we talking about?"

"Greta Golden. Her mother was June and her father's name was Aubrey."

Nanny held up a hand. "Didn't catch that. You're mumbling again."

Lucy repeated the names.

"Stop a minute. Canadian?"

"Yes."

"I remember her. I remember her because the nephew I was just joking about with you had just gone to Canada, year or two before, and I made her laugh by telling her I didn't know how he would get on because he couldn't even ride a horse, and she said he might not have to. I thought they were all cowboys out there. Or lumberjacks. But I've seen documentaries on the telly since, about Montreal and Toronto and the railway. And those wheat fields, hundreds of miles of them. Like Russia." She shivered. "Anyway, that's how I remember her. She got caught premature. As I remember it, she and her husband came over here for a little holiday before the baby was due, but she was advised to stay here because the birth was more advanced than they thought. So she signed in at Valleyfield. She would normally have had the doctor, but

being sort of a casual, and a foreigner, they arranged
for me to come because the doctor had four or five due
all at the same time. There was no problem, as I
remember. Little girl, wasn't it? Yes, Greta, you say."

"You remember the time?"

"Of course. I'm getting a bit hard of hearing but
I'm not potty yet. I remember it well. Besides, I've
already answered one lot of enquiries about this baby.
That refreshed my memory." Her mouth twisted into
a knowing pout as she watched Lucy's reaction. "Bit
surprised, are we? So now you tell me: who are you
and what are you after?" There was still no agression
in her question, just curiosity charged with the energy
from already having guessed the answer.

"I told you."

"That's all my eye. You're a detective, you are.
Like those on the telly."

Lucy lost her cool slightly and went pink. Later
she realized that it was her Ontario accent that made
her sound to a nanny from Cornwall like a private eye
from Los Angeles, like those on the telly.

"I'm being paid by Greta Golden to find out about
her birth," she said.

"That's what I thought. So you've found me and
I've told you what I've told you. Anything else? You
can come out in the open now. You want to know if she
had a birthmark on her bum? The baby, I mean. It
would have disappeared by now, anyway, most likely."

Lucy gave in. "Were you in the room the whole
time?"

"Yes. And I personally lifted Greta clear, washed
her, put a name tag round her ankle, and gave her to
her mother. She was sucking right away."

"Was the husband there?"

"He was in the lounge. I sent the nursing aide to tell him and he came up, kissed the mother and child, and left. I gave Mrs. Golden a cup of tea and waited until she was asleep. Then I put the baby in the crib and put my head down myself for five minutes in the next room. I came back early in the morning, checked them both, not just the name tag, but the whole baby as I always do because it doesn't take me more than a few minutes to get to know my babies. It was Greta all right. As a matter of fact she did have a small birthmark on the back of her head. Ask her if she still has it. So no one switched babies while I was in charge of her. If there was any switching it was after they left here."

"I'm sure nothing like that happened."

"You are *now*. You weren't though, when you walked in, were you? More tea?" Nanny grinned. "You'll have to come up with another plot, won't you," she added as she poured the tea.

"Do you know of anything else I might take back?"

"Well, there was the husband's death, of course. You know about that? She was still under my care then. I was glad baby had arrived, because a shock like that can give rise to problems."

"Do you remember anything about the accident?"

"Only that it was an accident, a fall off the cliff, while he was walking along the path with his sister-in-law."

"With who?"

"My patient's sister. She was staying at the inn in Rockingham Cove during the confinement. She visited every day with her boyfriend, but I think she left right after the inquest, with my patient. I don't know, really. Sad business, but nothing to do with what I was there for."

"Boyfriend? Did you meet him? What was he like?"

"Fair hair, a bit dopey like most of them. I never had to do with him. He waited in the sitting room. He drove them to London or wherever they went. It was his car, or one he'd hired, perhaps. Not so many people owned cars then."

"Who else did you tell all this to? You said ..."

"What was that?"

Lucy shouted her question again.

"That's better. Someone like you. A detective from London. I never saw him, but a clerk in the registry office told him about me. I know all those people in the town hall. Apparently he only wanted to verify the facts on the certificate, so he telephoned me. Just before you came."

"Was his name Michael Curnow?"

"I expect so. Now you'll have to come back again if you need to. I always spend half an hour with my bills now. More important to me than any shenanigans forty years ago."

There was a time, Lucy thought, when there was no problem getting the answer, at least in the classic fictions. But she knew what answer she would get now.

"Do you have the hotel register for 1957?" she asked the barman.

He laughed. "Don't be silly. Seriously, they'd have been stored for whatever length of time the law

requires for tax purposes, seven years probably, then
dumped. No. Why?"

"I'm trying to find the name of a couple who were
staying here then."

"Probably Smith. This is a nice quiet out-of-the-
way place. Lots of couples called Smith stayed here
then." He winked. "Those were the days, eh? Nowadays they'll sign in with two names even if they *are*
married. Women's lib."

Chapter Eighteen

That night, over a dinner of roast lamb, new pota-
toes, cauliflower, Brussel sprouts, and carrots —
which, though the most ordinary-looking item on the
menu, Curnow had urged her to order because, he
said, the elaborately cooked meals, of which there was
a lengthy list, were almost certainly shipped in from
Exeter frozen, and microwaved to order, whereas the
lamb would have been cooked on the premises — over
the dinner, then, Curnow had his own tale to tell.

"I found the coroner as he was then, long retired,
of course, in his seventies, I would think, but he didn't
have much trouble remembering the case and he
looked it up and went over it with me. First of all, have
you any idea who Golden was with when he fell?"

"Greta's aunt. Her mother's sister."

"How did you find out? Did you go to the local
paper?"

"I went to Nanny."

"Nanny who?"

"The midwife who delivered Greta."

"Right. Mrs. Barfield. I spoke to her myself. If it *is* Greta. Did you think of that?"

"Of course. It's Greta. There's a birthmark."

Curnow grinned. "There always is, isn't there? What interesting cases you Canadians get." He winked and took her closed hand in his and squeezed it.

Lucy took her hand away and patted his arm. "Tell me about the inquest."

"Right. Yes. The story goes like this. Aubrey Golden and his sister-in-law decided after dinner to go for a walk along the cliffs. It was cold and threatening rain so there was hardly anyone about. When they'd been gone about an hour, she came running back in a state, exhausted, crying, hands and knees bleeding from falling down, stockings torn, and she told the story. They'd simply gone to the edge to look down, she'd tripped slightly, he'd caught her, but she grabbed him like someone drowning, and he fell down. That was all right, but as they stood up his footing gave way and he went over the edge."

"This was the path we were on?"

"The coroner said it has stayed the same as long as he has known it. They get a lot of walkers along the cliffs, but not so many as to wear out the paths, like they do in the Lake District."

"Were there any witnesses?"

"Just one. A farm labourer on a tractor who was working on the field above the road saw the couple walking along the cliff, then a bit later he saw her running back along the road. Something fell out of her purse and he went down to pick it up, and go after her, but she had too good a start so he ran back up to the field and rode the tractor into Rockingham

Cove. He figured there was only one place she could be staying."

"What did he pick up?"Lucy asked.

"A book of travellers' cheques. American Express. He handed them in at the pub for safe keeping. They gave them back to the sister-in-law."

Lucy tasted a Brussel sprout and pushed it to one side. "What was the other man doing? There was another man with them, driving them about. Where was he?"

"Yes, Mrs. Barfield mentioned him when I telephoned. The sister's boyfriend, she called him. That's probably about it. Keeping her company."

"I wonder who he was, though."

Curnow snickered. "Orson Welles?"

"What?"

"*The Third Man*. Time he turned up, isn't it? I'm sorry, Lucy, but you get that dreamy look on your face and I know you're off again." Suddenly he jumped up. "Let's go for a walk," he said. "I'll show you the place."

"Not too near the edge."

They climbed up past the tennis court and followed the cliff path for half a mile. The sun was almost set but there was still plenty of light coming off the sea.

"See up there," Curnow pointed to the road that ran above them. "That's the farm that labourer was working on when he saw them."

They crossed the field to a stile set in a clump of bushes and came out of the bushes close to the edge of the cliff. It was as if someone had taken a giant bite out of the cliff, bringing the path too near the edge.

Lucy, vertigous, trod cautiously along the the cliff edge and looked down to the sea breaking over the rocks. "Hold on to me," she instructed Curnow, and stopped for a steadier look. Her foot slid an inch, and she screamed and hauled herself up to higher ground by using Curnow as a rope.

When she felt secure again, she forced herself to remember the last few sentences of their dinner conversation. "Did the labourer see them here? At this point?"

"He said not."

"So he didn't actually see them just before the incident."

"I suppose that's right."

"I wonder if he's still around. Everybody else seems to be."

"I've got his name. I'll ask at the pub. Are you okay?"

"Let's go up and walk back along the road. I don't mind it when the sun's shining, but it's getting dark."

"A nightcap?" Curnow suggested, diffidently.

"Sure," she said, and led the way to what she already thought of as their window.

Curnow brought two half pints of bitter from the bar. "The barman told me a young girl got swept off the rocks last week. It happens. I think that accidental death is not all that uncommon along any coast. You can't make the cliff safe for ... idiots, or protect people from tides."

"I'm certain it was an accident."

"No you're not. I am, but you aren't."

"Why would his sister-in-law want to kill him?"

"Surely you could find an answer to that, a smart detective like you?"

"Stop it. Perhaps he was just afraid of heights, like me. And ..."

"Perhaps she was just joking. Gave him a little push."

"We'll never know now, because the farm labourer never actually saw the incident, did he?"

"Not according to the inquest. More beer?"

"No thanks. I'm about ready for bed."

"Are you going to be all right? You still look a bit pale. I have some pills, if you want want one."

"No, no. I'll be fine."

"If you can bear with me a minute, there's something I want to say."

Lucy knew she had to cut this off immediately, but without inflicting any damage. "About Greta? I've changed my mind. Let's have the other half. What do I say? Same again?" She jumped up.

When she returned with the drinks and they had taken the first sip, he said. "Lucy, it's about being here with you I wanted to speak."

Lucy took a deep breath, and decided to play it for laughs, hoping he would get the point. "Michael, I must remind you. I'm spoken for, I told you."

The joke was awful; it came out exactly as if she meant it.

Curnow went scarlet and looked quickly round to see who might have heard them. "Keep it down, Lucy. I told you, it *was* about us I wanted to talk, but not like that. I just wanted to say that the last couple of days have been really — what's the word I want?"

"Smashing? You said that yesterday."

"Yes, well, now I've said it again." Suddenly the tension left, as he thought of a line which would say what he wanted without making it necessary for him to pack immediately. "Lucy, I haven't had such a pleasant couple of days since my wife died. I thought you should know that." He swallowed his drink and stood up. Lucy suspected that even having Nina around wouldn't help now. This wasn't what she had anticipated, and she was not at all prepared for it. She didn't know what to say.

"I don't know what to say," she said.

"You don't have to say anything. I just wanted to tell you that even if we go our ways tomorrow, I'll remember this."

"What? What will you remember?" Thus nearly dragging from him the thing she did not want to hear.

"You know what I'm talking about. Goodnight, Lucy."

Lucy had no idea what to do, and she guessed that she was going to have to wait until an older and more experienced Lucy could look back and tell her.

"Good night, Michael."

"Try the old vicar," the innkeeper suggested. "He's Methuselah himself, but his memory's all right. Could be he actually buried the bloke. Anyway, he's your best start."

Curnow said, "I suppose if you want to find out what happened forty years ago, then you are bound to run up against a lot of old people with good memories ..."

"In a village, yes," the barman said. "They're the ones who are left, except for holidaymakers."

The old vicar still lived in the old vicarage. The nearest and probably the quickest way would have been across the cliffs in the other direction from the scene of the accident, but Lucy had had enough of cliff walks for the time being. They drove about a mile back up to the highway and took the first lane to the left to bring them down to the little village church and rectory.

"They let me stay here in exchange for conducting the evening service," the vicar said. "Come in, come in."

He was a beautifully groomed and dressed little man with white hair which was just beginning to bend over the tops of his ears. In a week it might look shaggy, but at the moment it was no more than fashionable. Lucy wondered how he kept himself so immaculate — a tweed jacket, a lightly-checked brown flannel shirt, yellow wool tie, perfectly pressed grey trousers and the most exquisitely polished litle pair of brogues she had ever seen.

He led them through the hall into a sitting room where he had been reading the morning paper. "You're in luck, I've only got half an hour before my daughter comes to collect me. She's going in to Launceston and I have to get my hair cut. I've just had coffee, so I won't offer you any, if you don't mind. You see, if I don't go with her now, my daughter, I mean, I might have to wait another week by which time all seven of my parishioners will have noticed how long my hair is and wonder if I'm letting myself go." He screwed up his face in a tight little grin. "We're in a bit of a competition as to which one of us will lose our wits first. My housekeeper — well, that's a bit of a grand term, char-woman, really, because I still do my own cooking and I polish the furniture — I like doing that, whereas gardening, which I'm supposed to like, I hate. Now I don't know what you are here for but I assume it has to do with the church, so let's look at that and get it out of the way. Through here, then." He ducked through a door out to the garden, and waited for them to follow.

When they were assembled on the lawn, Curnow said, "It wasn't about the church ..."

"No? Oh, you've no idea what a relief that is. Let's go back inside." He took them back into the sitting room and pointed at some chairs. "But where was I, oh, yes, my charwoman says they watch me for the smallest sign of decrepitude." He grinned at them each in turn. "She insists on inspecting me before I begin a service to make sure I haven't forgotten my socks or something, so you see it's either now or never since I gave up driving myself — I'm eighty-four, but perfectly fit if you don't count one eye, nearly lost it because a fool of a surgeon bungled a cataract operation and I had to get it redone, but it's not the same. Point is, in the meantime I couldn't drive and now I don't want to; I rather like being driven about for anything important — people are very kind, so I never bothered even though the public transportation system — the local bus — has disappeared along with the destruction of most all the other country buses by that woman who ran us for all those years. The villagers had a better bus service in 1937 than they do now, so those less fortunate than I have reverted to ad hoc-ery, cadging rides from the neighbours, even from the local carter I shouldn't wonder, if he is willing.

You realize, of course, I'm just going on this pre-senile way to give you a chance to feel comfortable. Now, how can I help? Thinking of getting married, perhaps? Or seeking counselling?" Again he looked gleeful. "If that's the case you'll have to make an appointment with the incumbent rector for a Thursday afternoon. I don't do counselling."

Pity, Lucy thought. I could use some.

"Do you mind if I smoke?" he asked. "It *is* my house but the times again demand the question, as they did when I was a lad."

Lucy shook her head, curious to see if he had a miniature pipe, or a pack of tiny cigarettes. He took a small black cheroot from a tin and lit it with a wooden match which he carried loose in his pocket and struck on the sole of his shoe. "Dutch," he said. "The stogie." He smiled. "I smoke six a day for my health. Now we haven't got long. What is it to be?"

"Forty years ago a man was drowned off the cliffs near Rockingham Cove. His wife was in Shale having prematurely given birth to a daughter. He was walking with his sister-in-law, and he fell. The only witness was a farm labourer."

"No more." The vicar held up his hand. "Of course I remember. I did indeed bury the poor chap. Want me to look up the record? And I can tell you who the labourer was and is. We all live forever round here. Actually he's quite young to be retired, seventy, no more, but he's badly crippled with arthritis. George Faith his name is, and all he does nowadays is keep the grounds of that little church in Rockingham tidy. If you wait, I will persuade my daughter to lead us in a cavalcade to his cottage before we go to Launceston. Hardly out of her way."

As he finished, his daughter, a woman in her early sixties, could be seen and heard walking up the path, shouting. "Father! Father! Are you ready? Father! I'm in rather a hurry." She let herself in the front door of the vicarage. "Father!" she called again, for one final time before she walked into the sitting room. She smiled at Lucy briefly to counter any charges of rudeness, and turned to go back to the car.

"Just a minute, dear. We have to lead these people to George Faith's cottage. They've come from London to see him."

"Where is George Faith's cottage? I have a dental appointment for which I am already late." She turned to Lucy. "Not your fault. He always does this."

"If you'd just point the way ..." Lucy began.

"No, no, no, "the vicar interrupted. "You'll never find it in a million years. They are from Canada," he explained to his daughter.

The explanation quietened her, either by satisfying her or because she judged that it would be quicker to concede the point than to argue. Outside she started the car and crept forward slowly, waiting for Curnow to fall in behind her. They drove for three-quarters of a mile down a perfectly straight lane at the end of which a single cottage stood where another lane crossed theirs.

The daughter stopped, and the vicar got out of the car and trotted back to them. "That's it," he said, pointing to the cottage. "You'll be all right now. When you come back, follow that sign to Rockingham. Tell George I'll be up to see him tomorrow for a game of draughts. Cheerio."

"One more thing," Lucy called through the window. "Is there a funeral register? Like a marriage register? With the signatures of witnesses? Anything like that?"

"Nothing like that. Just a note in the church records, showing the clerical details, the money involved, that's all."

George Faith was in his garden behind the cottage, watching a cone-shaped pile of garden rubbish about four feet high, from the top of which a tiny white plume trailed out like a child's drawing of smoke. The labourer did not seem to have heard them. Lucy made to go forward, but Curnow clutched her arm. "He's making a bonfire," he said, reverently.

"Not much of one, is it?"

"It's perfect. Look at it. It'll burn like that for three days, then he will give it a tap and it'll all fall inward into a pile of ash no biggger than your fist." Curnow's hushed tone was suitable for describing a work of religious art.

"How do you know?"

"Because I've tried to make them. In my own garden. In Ilford. I can't do it. They don't even look like that to start. Then either they go out or the neighbours call the fire department. To make a proper bonfire, one like that, you have to be eighty years old and crippled with arthritis," he ended savagely.

After a final benediction in the form of a handful of grass laid across the top, George Faith turned away and saw them. "Ah," he said. "You come freggs?"

Lucy looked to Curnow for a translation. Curnow said, "The vicar told us to speak to you."

"Not freggs?"

"No."

"Then what do vicar want? Lost his key, did 'im?"

Lucy thought, he's sending us up. Nobody, not even here, still says "did 'im."

"What key?" Curnow asked.

"The church door. You wanted to see painting in church, did 'ee? Vicar's mislaid key again?"

"No, no. We're trying to find out about something that happened forty years ago." As Faith began to look bewildered, she continued. "A man drowned here, off the cliffs near Rockingham Cove. He was out walking. You saw them from a field above the road. Afterwards you picked up something that fell out of the woman's purse as she ran back to the inn."

Faith listened closely, watching the words emerge from her lips. When she stopped, he waited for a few seconds, then said, "Ah."

"You remember?"

"Ah."

"Could you tell us about it?" And don't say 'ah' again, she thought.

"Depends. Who are you?"

Lucy said, "I'm a friend of his daughter. The man who died. When I told her I was coming here on holiday she asked me to take some photos of the place where she was born, and where her father died. Then we got talking to people in Rockingham Cove and they said that the vicar who buried him was still alive and we just talked to him and he told us about you so I thought I might take your story back."

"I dug 'is grave, didn't I?"

"Did you? She'll be interested in that."

"Yeah. Oozee?"

"Mr. Curnow is a friend of mine."

"Oh, ah."

"Dad! They just want a chat. Ask them in." The voice came from behind them. Lucy turned to see a thin woman in rubber boots wearing thick-lensed glasses. "I'm his daughter," she said. "Audrey Lovelock. I look after him."

Lucy wondered if the whole of England was being looked after by its daughters. She put out her hand. "Lucy Trimble," she said. "And Michael Curnow."

"Come in. I'll make you a cup of tea."

The cottage had been arranged for George Faith's comfort, with no concessions to taste, style, or the original period of the building, which Lucy guessed was several hundred years before. It seemed to be made of stones, the walls thickly coated with plaster on the inside; the roof beam was like a huge railway tie with the original adze marks still visible. The floor, too, was made of stone, but mostly covered with linoleum and carpet. The furniture consisted of a three-piece suite of a kind Lucy remembered from her childhood, upholstered in a bristly carpet-like material that had now worn through to the canvas on the arms and across the top. Radiators supplied heat in winter; in the fireplace stood two televisions, one on top of the other.

By the time the daughter came out of the kitchen with a tray of tea, Lucy had heard most of the story of the cottage from Faith ("It were moi faather's and 'is faather's afore 'im and back and back to Napoleon. Oi put in the central 'eating, though, and the tellies, and the fridge, and the microwave") and they were ready to hear his account of Golden's death.

"The first oi knew was I was wiring up the fence in the top pasture, for to keep the sheep from straying."

Lucy said, "The court said you were on a tractor."

"That's right. I was sort of patrolling the fence, loike, looking for any breaks. It was a bit windy, and not too warm so I was hoping to finish up soon, before the rain got 'eavy like, and I looked down and seen them on the bluff, 'im and 'er." He sucked at his tea. "Then they was hid behind a clump of bushes and then I caught her again out of the corner of me oi, runnin' back along the path by 'erself. Even from so far as I was I could see she was upset, then I saw something drop out of her bag so I started down after 'er, but by the time I got across the road and down the meadow she was halfway to the inn, so I picked up what she'd dropped and drove back on the tractor to leave it at the pub Rockingham."

"The travellers' cheques."

"Ah, that's it. They was the first I'd ever seen so I didn't recognize what they was, but they 'ad 'er name on 'em."

"You remember her name?"

"No."

"Turley?"

"It don't ring a bell."

"Did you testify at the inquest?"

"I did."

"Just as you told us now?"

The man looked up and wiped a trace of spittle from below his bottom lip, then glanced at his daughter, who nodded at him.

"Oi didn't testify to everything I saw. That was nobody's business, I thought."

Lucy held her breath. Audrey, slightly excited, said. "It was forty years ago. You can tell Mrs. Trimble now. She will know if she should tell the daughter in Canada."

"They was kissing and cuddling. Loike a honeymoon couple."

After a bit, Lucy said, "Did they stop? Sit down? Lie down?"

"Course not," Faith exploded. "They stayed standing with their arms reund each other."

"How far away were you?"

"Two fields and a road."

"It wasn't a clear evening, you said. A bit of rain."

"That's right. But they *was* cuddlin'. Goin' at it."

"And you didn't testify to this at the inquest."

"It weren't nobody's business. Afterwards I surmised that a man and his sister-in-law was very happy that a baby was born, a daughter for him, a niece for her."

Lucy put down her cup. "I'm sure you're right."

"Oi could show you the place. We could go up in your car."

"We were up there yesterday. The coroner gave us directions. No, thanks. You've been very good with your time. One last thing. The other man staying with them at the inn, do you remember his name?"

"No, but I do remember that he weren't staying at t'inn. He come for her every morning."

"Do you know where he was staying?"

"Ah. A bed and breakfast farmhouse up by Trevarne."

"Thanks, Mr. Faith. Now, we have to go. Michael?"

"Right." Curnow stood up. "One thing, Mr. Faith. He pointed to where he had been watching through the window. "How long will you keep the bonfire going?"

"Three or four days should do it, oi reckon."

Curnow nodded, satisfied.

Lucy said, "Can I ask a personal question, too? Why do you have two television sets like that?"

"Everybody asks that," the daughter said. "It's for the racing. On Saturday afternoons he tunes in to both channels so he can catch all the races at the different courses. Don't you?" she said to her father, shouting suddenly, angry. "Turn them on. Saturday afternoons. For the racing."

"Ah."

Chapter Nineteen

Outside, before they got into the car, she said, "What did you think of that?"

"I wasn't listening too hard, Lucy. I was watching the bonfire."

Patiently she repeated what Faith had said, and pointed out the implications.

Curnow said, "It's a can of worms. Leave it alone."

"Why? They're all dead. Nobody's going to get hurt now."

"I don't know. Makes me uneasy in case I should be considering the possible consequences for my clients."

"Why?"

"I don't *know*," Curnow said. "I'm trying to think of any. But if Golden was into a little hanky-panky with his sister-in-law while his wife was in the maternity home, so what? They were just making the world go round."

"You don't sound as if you approve, though. But supposing they weren't? Supposing he ... made a pass at her on the cliff?"

"Bloody hell, Lucy, now you're back in Victorian days. You mean he put his hand up her skirt and what Faith saw was ..."

"Him embracing, her struggling."

"You mean?" He assumed an expression of mock horror, the back of his hand to his brow.

"All right, all right. But did that coroner say anything about this. Did the hanky-panky come out in court?"

"What came out in court was the story of an accident, which it was. Sad, but an accident."

"Where was the sister-in-law staying?"

"Where else? There's just the pub."

"And him? Golden?"

"The same place, I would think. Like us."

"Why? Why weren't they both staying in Shale, near the maternity home?"

"God love us, Lucy, they came here because it's *nice* here. Shale is probably a dead-and-alive hole after the shops shut. This, though, is a holiday place. Seaside. Bit wild, and not a lot to do, but some people like that, and it's always jolly in the bar." They turned into the parking lot of the pub.

Lucy said, "I see. So the three of them, June Turley and her husband, and her sister, Rose, all came to Rockingham Cove for a holiday, in December."

"That's it. A little break for June."

"Then June came on suddenly and was rushed into Shale where she had her baby prematurely?"

"Probably."

"Then her husband went for a walk with Rose and fell off the cliff?"

"Something like that."

"Then June came back to Canada with the baby, Greta, and never spoke to her sister again?"

"Is that right?"

"I don't believe a word of it. Rose killed him because he made a pass at her while her sister was only just out of labour. It's obvious. Then she went back and told her sister, but June didn't believe her and told her never to come near her or the baby again. That's what happened. Aubrey Golden was a pig."

"Lucy, what you're thinking would have occurred to the coroner, wouldn't it? But he never said a word about it yesterday. Open and shut, black and white — that was his attitude."

"But you didn't actually ask him, did you?"

"I didn't know, did I?"

"I think I'll ask him. Will you drive me into Shale?"

"I will, but I won't come in with you. He'll think me a bloody nuisance."

But there was no need to go to Shale. As they entered the lounge, the barman said, "Mrs. Trimble, message for you." He handed over a slip of paper. The message read, "I'm coming in to the pub for lunch at twelve. Would you wait for me and give me a few minutes of your time?" It was signed, "Henry Carpenter."

"Who is Henry Carpenter?" she asked the barman. "Do you know him?"

Curnow interrupted. "That's the old coroner I've been telling you about. Let's have a glass of beer and wait for him. It's five to the hour now. Oh dear, oh dear, he sounds as if he might have a bone to pick with us."

Henry Carpenter appeared as they were sitting down, introduced himself, shook hands with both of them, and sat down.

He was very tall and very thin, with a thick fringe of hair surrounding a bald sun-burned crown. He wore a striped silk scarf knotted in the open neck of a white shirt, an old blazer, also striped, with a badge on the pocket.

"Cyril!" he called. "Bring me a large gin, would you. And a pasty. Make it three?" He raised an eyebrow and Lucy and Curnow nodded. "And take their drink orders, would you? You have? Good."

"You know the barman?" Lucy asked.

"Never seen him before in my life. This isn't my local, I'm sorry to say. Nice pub."

"But you know his name."

"Haven't the faintest idea. The problem is in this country, and for all I know in yours, there is no equivalent to the European 'Garcon!' or clapping your hands in Spain. Here you're reduced to trying to catch his eye, sitting with your head on backwards for as long as he cares to ignore you, then nodding and grinning and pointing at your glass like an alchoholic deaf-mute, even if it's a sandwich you want. I decided after long hard thought that calling them all 'Cyril' is the right answer. It implies that you are temporarily confusing this barman with some other, perhaps his predecessor who *was* called Cyril. Most probably it only works when you've reached seventy-five and you can get away with damn near anything. They just think you're a silly old fool who's forgotten where he is, but you get your drink."

"Why 'Cyril'?"

"Cyril is a name without associations. It doesn't imply that you are patronizing him. 'Charlie' for instance, might sound as if you are slightly taking the mickie. You know, 'a real Charlie'? And Herbert is worse."

By now Cyril had appeared with the food, which Carpenter insisted on paying for, and they began to sip and munch. The Cornish pasties were hot and tasty, and Lucy wanted to ask why they were peculiar to the region but she feared inspiring another monologue. Instead, she said, "How did you know we were here?" This seemed politer than asking him what he wanted.

"George Faith," Carpenter answered. "George's daughter, Audrey — now *there*'s a name we could talk about, she telephoned me to say that a Canadian woman was enquiring after the death of a man named Golden, forty years ago. Now I can see on your faces that you think it is surprising that she should be alerting me in this way. Nothing sinister. Not even significant. Point is, she is my gardener, she works for me for three afternoons a week, and she was just telephoning to say she would be a bit late today and why. You had held her up. Small world, isn't it? But when I heard what you were interested in, I thought we had better have a word." He held up his paper napkin. "Are we finished? Then let's drive up to where George Faith saw the couple on the cliff."

They used Carpenter's car, and went up into the village, then turned south along the narrow road above the cliffs. On the left the fields were cultivated, but the land on the cliff side was National Trust property, preserved for the people. Carpenter drove along for over a mile, the road twisting and doubling back on itself with the contours of the land. "I saw you were looking at my trainers," he said, as they drove along the road above the cliff. "Have you tried them yourselves? My wife made me buy a pair. I thought they were a kind of plimsolls, at first. You remember plimsolls? They certainly aren't. The greatest advance in footwear since wellingtons. I've been wearing clogs for the past couple of years. I like clogs because they work like pattens. You know about pattens? Those wooden shoes people used to leave outside the kitchen door so as not to bring mud into the house. I like clogs for that because I have a big garden, and I'm out there most of the time. It's a damned nuisance when the phone rings to have to take off your wellies before you can answer it. Same with calls of nature. So I wear clogs at home to stay above the mud and kick them off when I go indoors, but for a bit of a hike, or a stroll along the cliffs, as we are going to do now, clogs are tricky if you weren't born in them.

"An American lady came along wearing these and I thought they were very unbecoming, made her look lumpen. The thing was, the rest of her was very becoming, indeed, so I thought if she was prepared to look like a bog-wader from the ankles down, there must be something in them. My wife tried a pair first, and she was bowled over — bowled over. So I got meself a pair. Now I wear only these and clogs. The rest of my shoes gather dust in the closet, waiting for me to be invited to the palace."

Just past a sign directing travellers to a bed-and-breakfast lodging, Carpenter pulled into a parking area which had been carved out of the side of the road. A police notice warned that thieves ransacked cars regularly.

"Aren't you going to lock it?" Curnow asked.

"No, and I'm going to roll the window down slightly. Now no one has to break in to find I've left nothing of value in the car, and the fact that it is unlocked implies that I am behind the wall, having a pee. The police don't agree, but I've had no trouble so far. Now, we climb up here and walk along about fifty yards. Now, this is the point where we climb up a couple of furrows to overlook the scene. Now look. That is what George Faith saw. Perfect."

They looked down the meadow towards the sea and saw a couple, a man and a woman, walking along the cliff path, just far enough away so that their faces were unrecognizable.

"Watch," Carpenter said. The couple disappeared below an outcropping of rock covered in low bushes, stayed out of sight for several minutes, then reappeared fifty yards farther along and lower down.

"Were these stone walls here then?" Lucy asked.

"For at least a hundred years," Carpenter said. "What you see now is exactly what Faith saw in 1958. Let's go down and take a closer look," he said, leading them across the road to the wall on the other side. "See, behind those bushes the cliff falls away to a sheer drop. That is where it happened. A little while after they went behind those bushes, George Faith saw her reappear. He realized she was in trouble because she was running hard. He shouted and started down the meadow, but she didn't hear anything."

"He saw her drop something, though. The travellers' cheques."

"That's right. So he collected them and came back up to his tractor, drove into Rockingham and left them at the pub. With Cyril's predecessor. Now let's go down below."

The path opposite the parking space took them across to the cliff walk which they followed to where it dipped below the clump of bushes. There it took an elbow shape and it was possible to look down through the crook of the elbow and see the rocks pounded by the sea below. "Not much chance of surviving a fall down there, wouldn't you say?"

Lucy stayed as far back as she could while trying to see beyond the edge. She reached out for Curnow's hand and held onto him firmly to creep a little closer. Carpenter strolled to within an inch of the edge and kicked at a piece of cliff which broke away and fell for a long time before disintegrating on the rocks below. A man on the beach looked up.

"'Gathering samphire, dreadful trade,'" Carpenter said.

Lucy had retreated six or eight feet. "What's 'samphire'?"

"I've no idea. Something you gather on cliffs. The quotation is from *King Lear.* It's about heights, really. Seen enough? Let's go back to the harbour. Did you notice the little beach restaurant opposite the pub? They make good coffee. Even Americans like it. And tea, too."

Chapter Twenty

"Why are you taking all this trouble?" Lucy asked when they were seated in the little harbour square, watching two boys surfboarding. From his opening monologue, she had been sceptical that they were getting the entirely unaffected Carpenter. She had caught a glimpse of something very early, a watchfulness behind the jolly patter which had continued all through the excursion on the cliff and was in place even now. Carpenter, she felt sure, was concerned about something.

"I could ask you the same question. And that would be my answer. 'Why are you so curious about an accident that took place forty years ago?'"

Lucy explained her mission once more. "And that's all it was. Just filling in the details in a friend's family history. Until George Faith told us what he saw on the cliff path."

"Two people embracing. Congratulating each other on the birth of a child."

"That's what I said then," Curnow agreed. "Now

I'm not so sure. When I talked to you yesterday, you never mentioned this."

"Why would I?"

Curnow, a terrier now, smelling a rat, said, "Did George Faith testify at the inquest?"

"He did."

"About the embracing part?"

"He never mentioned it."

"Why?"

"He said it was nobody's business."

"Did you go along with that?"

"Yes, I did." Carpenter was no rat to be shaken in Curnow's teeth. "I'll tell you why, shall I? First of all it is a coroner's duty to determine the cause of death, as quickly and as certainly as he can. He does not have to call an inquest, if he is satisfied that he knows what happened. In this case, a very sad business, you will agree, I saw no reason to question the obvious. George Faith's story of the couple kissing and cuddling as he put it, gave me pause, at first. But you know George Faith is and always was a puritan. That would be the polite term. We don't *know* what he saw. What he reported was his interpretation. Farm labourers here are very conservative, politically and morally — read Bernard Shaw on the subject; you or I might have reported seeing something quite different, something, I am sure, entirely innocent."

Curnow could not let go easily. "Supposing it wasn't?"

"Suppose it was carnal, you mean? While his wife groaned in labour, as the tabloids would put it."

"That's what I wondered."

"Consider what then? Would it have any bearing? The death was still an accident, whatever lay behind the embrace. Surely, either interpretation, mine, or dirty-minded George's, reinforces that. It was an accident."

Lucy said, "So, what you are saying is, 'Why drag this into the inquest, since it is only innuendo and wouldn't change the verdict?'"

"Now you're there."

"So you told George Faith not to mention it."

"That I couldn't do, legally and because that would strengthen his idea that he had seen something interesting. I just kept my questions as straightforward as possible. I never let him stray off the path."

"Then why did you call an inquest? You don't have to, you said?"

"It seemed to be expected. And I judged it the simplest way of putting the question to rest."

"To demonstrate that it was an accident? Then why are you so concerned about us?"

"Because, madam, as I understand it, you are two private detectives, and one of you ..." he looked at Curnow "... might have an interest in the possibility that it wasn't an accident. That being the case, you might feel it is in your client's interest to go to the police and cause a lot of gossip involving the coroner's office. So I thought I would tell you that before I conducted the inquest I thought very hard about my duty, as I hope you will about yours, and I had a word with the police — not the local constable, but the man who would have been given the problem of whether to investigate and he agreed that since there was simply no possibility of confirming or denying the woman's testimony, there being no witnesses as to what took place at the point on the cliffs where he fell, then we had to accept her word. There was no reason at all why not. And further, when I leave here, I shall get in touch with that policeman's successor and confirm that, in spite of the presence of you two asking questions, his predecessor's judgement was sound. Now. What are you going to do?"

"Nothing," Curnow said immediately. "Nothing at all. Perfectly satisfied. That's all we wanted to see you about. One thing, though, more your concern than ours, George Faith must have said the same to other people."

"Probably, but not immediately. He was the star of the inquest, you see, and he enjoyed that, and later I had a little chat with him about malicious gossip. That kept him quiet until the press went away. Aubrey Golden was just a tourist who fell off a cliff, and that's bad for the holiday trade, so most people would want to sweep the thing under the carpet, or, in this case, out to sea."

"Fair enough," Curnow said.

"*Is* it, Mr. Curnow? Fair enough?"

"Oh, yes, yes. You won't hear from me again."

As Carpenter stood up, Lucy said, "Would it make any difference to the way you think if I told you that the two sisters never spoke to each other again."

"Why didn't they?"

"I don't know."

"Nor will you. So, no. That may be an interesting part of the story of two sisters. It's not part of the inquest."

Lucy smiled, nodded in understanding, shrugged, and said, "It's time I thanked you for your patience and courtesy, and ... and the lunch. You've been very polite. No more questions, but I think I might stay in the area for a couple more days. Perhaps you could point me to some of the local beauty spots. Let me walk down to the parking lot with you, and get my map. Michael, order me another coffee, would you? I'll be right back."

Thus Lucy got a few moments alone with Carpenter. Standing by her car, holding the map in case Curnow was watching, she said, "One more thing."

Carpenter sighed. "The sister-in-law. You'd like to talk to her yourself."

"Not because I'm not satisfied."

"Then why?"

"I am over here to put together the story of my client's birth, part of her history, and now I've learned that her aunt was there when she was born. She might still be alive. I'd like to talk to her. Perhaps she would have something to add."

"Then ask her, why don't you?"

"I don't know where to find her. Can you give me a start?"

"There will be an address in the records, but it won't do you much good. I mean — it's forty years old!"

"It's the only lead I have."

"Telephone me at home, tonight."

"Thank you. Now put some crosses on my map to mark the beauty spots. My colleague is still watching."

"A little friendly rivalry."

"Sort of. And he's a nag." As she was folding the map, she added, "I agree it doesn't make much difference, or any difference, but what do you think George Faith saw?"

"I think he saw two people embracing."

"Carnally? as you put it, or — is there a word? — like in-laws?"

"No, no. You have to fold it like a concertina. Here, let me. There. You'd want to consult a sociologist on the history of body language, what gestures meant forty years ago, what they mean now. In the meantime I think I can tell you that forty years ago you did not casually embrace your sister-in-law on top of a cliff, even if you were very happy. You might give her the odd hug if you had known her a long time, but casual hugging is a fairly new thing that everybody started doing about twenty years ago. Fifty years ago people came back from the war and got a nice kiss from sisters-in-law, and I think that was still true ten years later. So if you are asking me, I'd say those two were embracing."

"Just as George Faith said."

"Not quite. Now we are at the nub of it, what George Faith thought he saw. Now George Faith thought he saw them making love."

"Going at it ..."

"What!"

"That's the phrase he used to us."

"Exactly. A no that is what he would have said in court if I had encouraged him. But what dirty-minded George Faith thought he saw, and what was really happening may have been very different."

"No one would have believed him surely. I mean, literally? Standing up in the rain?"

"Oh, yes. A couple of the lads in my platoon during the war came from Liverpool; they called it 'having a knee-trembler.' Quite common, then, apparently."

She felt a warning in his salty speech, an edge. "I see. And you were afraid that George's story was more interesting than the truth?"

"That's the idea. That's what I thought. I was concerned to avoid idle speculation. I still am. Even if George was right, what difference does it make, except to a lot of gossip mongers? The situation stayed the same; nothing was provable. Think about that before you rush home with a story. Phone me at home tonight for that address."

Back in the bar, she said to Curnow, "So what do you make of it?" partly to see what he thought, but also to keep away his own questions.

"You mean why is he going to all this trouble for you? Because he's on a cover-up. That's why."

"Covering up a mistake he made forty years ago?"

"Perhaps not a *mistake*. A decision, more like it. As he says. But he doesn't want anyone like us to go behind it now, so he's frightening us off."

"Frightening?"

"Frightening. Reminding me he's in touch with the constabulary. That kind of thing. Works, too. You heard me back off. I'm satisfied."

"Frightened?"

"Bloody right. This isn't Canada, Lucy. A private investigator's licence here is hard to get, and it means something. Now what that beanpole was saying as he fixed me with his beady eye was, 'Any trouble from you, old cock, and you'll find renewing your licence won't be so easy. You'll find it's been endorsed, or whatever the equivalent is.' So I said, 'Right your are, sir, three bags full, sir. No further trouble from me, sir.'"

"You were quite aggressive at first."

"I forgot myself because I smelled the fox. Now, Lucy, let's pack it in, go for a walk, no, go for a ride, have a bit of dinner here, then tomorrow farewell. How about it?"

"No."

"No, *what*?"

"There's something fishy. I'm going to have another chat with Nanny."

"Don't you ever stop? All right, go and see Nanny. I'm going to have a kip. Wake me when you come back."

Nanny said, "You never asked. You have now, so I'll tell you. When the police came with the news, she took it calmly enough. I was afraid she might go into shock, but her sister arrived soon after and *she* was the one in shock, I reckon. And she went in with Mrs. Golden and baby and they closed the door on me. She came out an hour later, looking as if she'd been crying her eyes out, but Mrs. Golden was very calm. The only effect I noticed was that she lost her milk and we had to switch baby to a bottle. The next day she said that she wanted to be discharged as soon as possible and I was to go out and buy everything necessary for bottle-feeding — everyone's gone back to nature lately, I notice, but in those days bottle-feeding was the norm. So I went to the shops and got ready a travel kit so that she could feed baby for up to twenty-four hours if she had to. A week later, her sister fetched her in a car and they drove up to London."

"London? You sure?"

"That's how I remember it, and why would I remember it wrong? That's where they came from, and they went back there."

"When was the funeral?"

"I can't remember. They buried him as soon as the coroner released him, I think. By the way, does she still have webbed toes? Her dear little second and third toes were joined together when she was born, and that's the only case I ever had like that, though I've heard of it with others since."

"I'll ask her." And that, thought Lucy, by the laws of probability, should finally settle that.

Curnow was still sleeping when she got back. Although it was still only late afternoon, she phoned the coroner, apologized for the earliness of the call, and got the old Cambridge address for Greta's aunt, then asked him about the other man. Had the coroner had reason to record his name?

"As I remember, he helped identify the body."

"Did you keep a record?"

"Of course."

"May I know it?"

"It is in my office, which is locked up." He paused. "But it's only downstairs, so I'll unlock it when I have had my dinner, find what you want and leave a message at your hotel. All right?"

"I'm very grateful."

"Hands across the sea, that's me," he said, and hung up.

She called Greta at home and reported all she had

learned from the coroner and Nanny. She finished by asking Greta about her toes — were the second and third ones joined? Webbed? They were. Lucy wondered if that would be called circumstantial evidence. "Then, you are certainly your mother's daughter, and nobody switched you in the cradle which was a possible loophole they might have held you up with. Now I'm coming home. I'll try to get a seat on the Air Canada flight tomorrow."

"Lucy, Lucy, Lucy. Isn't my money any good? Can't you stay a couple more days? Please. Go to Cambridge. Find my aunt and take her picture. My God, she really might still be there. My only living relative. My family! Never mind this inheritance thing. If you do find her, call me right away."

"What do you know about her? Anything?"

"She worked for a publisher here. She was a proofreader. That's not a proper job, though, is it? She must be doing something else now, if she's alive. But listen. I've been doing some sleuthing, too. I'm still trying to find out if anyone remembers the doctor who might have done the blood test when they got married. What? I told you, he might know if Daddy was impotent, I mean sterile. I'll find someone. Call me when you find out anything."

Half an hour later, while Lucy was having a nice nap, a call came from the coroner. He had had to open the office for something else and he had looked up the name of the identifying witness. It was James McSweeney.

Chapter Twenty-one

Fresh cod was on the menu again, so they both ordered it, not knowing when they would be offered it again.

"I remember my father telling me once that it was like this during the war," Curnow said. "fish wasn't rationed, but it was in short supply. I think most of the North Sea trawlers had been converted to minesweeping. Anyway, suddenly, outside a Fish and chip shop, the sign would go up, 'Frying Tonight,' and we would put away the packet of dried egg, or whatever we had planned for dinner, and rush out to line up for rock salmon and chips. So what did Nanny have to say?"

Lucy recounted her conversation with Nanny, adding, "I called Greta while you were asleep. She wants me to find out if her aunt is still alive."

"Finally, I come into my own. What do you know? What's her name?"

"Rose Turley. But she might have married."

"Address?"

"It's somewhere in Cambridge." She gave him the address.

"That's a start, a good one, too. It looks like a street address, a house, I mean, not a hostel or something like that. That means there might still be neighbours who remember her. So, let's go to Cambridge. Ill get my map and we'll have a look at it after dinner."

Lucy lifted her purse off the floor. "Here. I've still got my map with me."

"Let's have a look. What are these crosses?"

"Beauty spots. The coroner put them on. I won't be able to see them now, but Michael, *we* aren't going anywhere. You are going home to your little girl. I am going to Cambridge."

He laughed. "You don't know anything about finding a missing person in this country, or probably in Canada, either. Someone's got to show you. Besides, where did you plan to leave me off. Exeter? And then I suppose you were just going to look at the map and jog across England, were you? Have you ever tried to drive across England? Can't be done. No. We go M5, M4, M25, and M11. We could do it by tomorrow night."

"No, we don't. I'm not going on those damn M roads. I'm not in a rush. I want to see a bit more of England while I'm here. Dartmoor, at least."

He sighed. "All right. Over to Launceston, then — you could buy a pair of clogs, prove you've been away — then to Princetown — Dartmoor, to you — and then we head for the A30 to Salisbury, then up ..."

"Clogs," she interrupted him. "What was all that about clogs when we first met Mr. Carpenter?"

"I told you. He was blowing smoke. Doing the charming old cove bit. But I was watching his eyes, like

I said, and *he* was watching you. He was talking just to cover up that he was sizing you up. Clever old sod. And that's one more reason why I won't tangle with him."

"That's what I thought. Salisbury it is, then. Then what?"

"Then we have to go on to the M3, like it or not. It's not sensible to do anything else. We have a look at Stonehenge, then straight up."

"Why can't we stay the night in Winchester?" she said, pointing. "I've heard of that."

"We *could* do that, yes ..."

"And from there, see, it's straight up to Oxford. We could drive through Oxford at least, and then cross over to Cambridge."

Patiently, he shook his head. "The trip from Oxford to Cambridge takes six hours through the most boring part of England. It's all little shoe factories and housing estates and market gardens. Give in. All roads lead to London and that's the way we'd better go. Take my word for it."

"All right. But we have to stop the car at Dartmoor prison. Actually turn the engine off."

"Promise."

"But Michael, I have to say it again. Why are you taking all this trouble for me?"

"I just want to be there when we find out the last detail of this sodding story. See, my client would like me to find that what happened forty years ago was very fishy, so they can challenge the will. So far there's nothing doing. Your client is the legal heir, all right. But now we find out there was some hanky-panky on the cliff-top needs explaining. It doesn't make any difference, I tell myself, but it looks funny in my report. So at the end, my report says, 'Mrs. Trimble proceeded to Cambridge, but I could see no reason to accompany her.' I've told you what these people are like; they'll never be satisfied as long as there's a chance that something else happened. They'll want to be dead sure."

"Leave all that out. Everything about me. Tell them you interviewed the coroner, and that was that."

"They'll hire someone else to go over the same ground, and it will look as if I didn't do my job properly. I'd better come with you."

"I must do one thing before we go. Let me have a word with Cyril."

She had just remembered her promise to get a message to Johnny. The barman was happy to send a fax on the inn's machine, and Lucy wrote out a message for Peter Tse to pass on that she would be in Cambridge for two or three days, then she would fly home. Even as she composed it she was aware that she was feeding an uneasiness to which she did not want to give a name. The fact that she was not sure whether to bother sending the fax told her that she was not sure about anything else.

"By the way," Michael said, when she came back to the window, "Just so you won't think I've been holding out on you, when I came back from Canada that time, I strolled round to Manor Park, to a pub there called the Three Rabbits. I picked up a whisper about Geoffrey Golden there. It's true he was a used car dealer, but that term covers a lot in Manor Park. In Geoffrey's case it covers the fact that all the cars he dealt in were stolen, although he was only actually convicted of possession. But he did time for assault and GBH, and he was suspected of half the robberies around Ilford. I knew the name registered, first time I heard it. He was a major villain was our Geoffrey. The whole family was sticky-fingered."

"Including Aubrey? Maybe that's why he went to Canada — he was on the run. Then it all caught up with him?"

"What? All what? For Christ's sake, Lucy, Aubrey they remembered as the exception. He lived with his aunt in Chelmsford who took him in because there were too many living in the house. Aubrey even went to a grammar school. I think he almost certainly went to Canada because he was bored with Manor Park, and he wanted to get away from his dysfunctional family."

"Is that why they are so hostile?"

"Now there I am with you. The word among the knowledgeable in the Three Rabbits was that by the time he was sixteen he thought himself too good for them, which he probably was. They think his daughter's got a nerve claiming the family money."

Lucy laughed. "It *is* the Magwich story, but this time Pip emigrated. Good night Michael."

They did stop at Princetown, and looked at the prison, but they never left the car. "It's sort of tamer than I imagined," Lucy said.

"I would think most things are. The sun's too strong today. We should come back when they can promise a mist."

"Those cells are only nine feet by five," Lucy said. And then, even in bright daylight, the true idea of the place came through to her and she shivered. "Let's go, then. I've seen it."

"There's a good pub at the crossroads," Curnow said. "If we can get there before the German and Japanese buses arrive, we can get a sandwich and sit outside."

They beat the rush and collared seats outside where they ate some bread and cheese, each plate garnished with two giant spring onions, like leeks.

"You not eating yours?" Curnow enquired, transferring them to his own plate and chomping away at each of them in turn like a rabbit in a cartoon. While he was finishing them off, Lucy called home. First she called the stables at the track, because at seven in the morning he could well be there already, if he had a horse he was concerned with. The stable girl told her he was at home, so she called the farm. There being no answer there, she called the apartment and there he was. Quickly, to keep the cost down, she told him what she was doing and when she might be home, and got a vague, "Great, great," in reply, and "See you," and then, in the background, from the other side of the bed, someone laughed. Lucy kept her head, said, "'Bye, then," and returned to their bench outside.

She was too well prepared by the hints that had gone before to be shattered, but she was shaken. At the same time she felt a little light-headed, already experiencing the relief that from here on it would be all right. Because it was over, there was no question about that. She had not known how she would react when she confirmed her fears, but now her response was immediate and final. She would survive, was already surviving, and she would be careful in future. No, she wouldn't. She would still take all the chances she had to, but now she would know she was taking chances.

"Good news, Lucy?"

She looked up at Curnow who was watching her from across the table. "What? No. Why?"

"You were smiling."

"I do that. It doesn't mean anything. At school my teachers used to think I was making fun, when I was just trying to make my face the way they wanted it."

"What are you talking about?"

"Nothing. I think the prison got to me. Could we go?"

On the road to Exeter. Lucy said, "I like Dartmoor. The moor, I mean. I think the muskeg in northern Canada must look like this, only not so pretty. Could we stop?"

Curnow found a layby almost immediately, and Lucy got out and walked away, turning her back on Curnow who stayed by the car. A few yards from the car, she stopped, safely alone, and looked across the moor. A few minutes was all she needed. When she returned, Curnow silently let her back into the car and offered her a mint from the supply they had bought. She took it, and leaned across the seat and kissed him on the cheek. "Thanks," she said.

An hour later they were across the moor.

"There's a place I know just before we get to Salisbury," he said. "We could have a cup of tea there. All right?"

They found Stonehenge and joined the tourists who swarmed over the site.

"I'm afraid you have to come in the middle of the winter if you want to see it without all these people," he said.

"That's all right. The stones are still there."

They ate an ice cream and came down to Salisbury where they spent ten minutes in the cathedral, driven out by the organist who was practising scales very slowly at ear-shattering volume.

"Why is he doing that when the place is full of people?" Lucy shouted over the din at a man in a dog collar. "It's a kind of torture."

"God knows," the cleric said. "*I* don't work here, thank Heavens. I think he's just showing off. I agree. Hellish, isn't it?"

Curnow asked, finally, "Anything wrong? You don't usually shout at people."

"Not with you, Michael," she said. "But let's get out of here. Could we get to Cambridge tonight?"

"Late."

"All right. We'll make an early start tomorrow."

They stayed the night in Winchester; the next day they hurtled grimly along the M roads, stopping once for a second breakfast at a service station (a second breakfast, Curnow explained, because it's the meal they can't bugger up). Late in the afternoon, Curnow led them through Cambridge into the car park by the market square.

"It's three o'clock now," Curnow said, when they were drinking tea in a café off the square. "Let's go down to the Tourist Bureau — it's just in the next street — and get a couple of rooms. Then you go for a walk, have a look round — I'll show you where — and I'll see what I can find out. All right?"

"It might take you days to find out anything."

"And it might not." He winked. "Let's go."

But when they found rooms at a two-star hotel ("It's all on expenses," Curnow said), Lucy lost any desire for sight-seeing. "I'm going to the hotel," she said. "I'll meet you in the bar at six."

She felt slightly sad as she made her way to the hotel. Here she was in one of the most famous and lookable-at cities in the world and what she craved was a cup of coffee, a bath, and a nice read, which she hadn't had for a week. It was a function of her age that one of the pleasures of travelling was not travelling, stopping for a bit, lying down.

The room was nice, furnished agreeably enough and with a comfortable bed, a big bathtub, and a tray of tea-makings. Half an hour later she was lying in the tub, drinking tea and trying to keep Reginald Hill dry.

Chapter Twenty-two

Michael woke her at six-thirty from a little doze begun two hours before. "Right down," she shouted. "Watch stopped."

She made it to the bar in fifteen minutes. "I was writing letters," she said, "Lost track of the time."

"The side of your face is all creased from the bedspread."

"Yes? I was writing lying down. What did you find out?" she asked. She sipped the tiny, not-very-cold gin-and-tonic he had ordered for her, finding it, as usual, both in size and flavour much more to her taste than the North American version.

"Everything," he said. "Rose Turley is still alive. She still lives here. I have the address; we're going see her tomorrow."

"You've seen her? Greta's aunt? You sure it's her? She's been living here for forty years, and not a word? My God. What's she like?"

"No. Yes. Yes. Yes. Don't know. Want to know how I found her?"

"All right. It's something I need to learn, I suppose, but hurry it up."

"It's often quite a bit easier in a place like this, because fragments of older communities have survived, like little villages, never mind the motorways and the glass towers. There are streets of working-class cottages, many of them tarted up by academics and such ..."

"White-painted?"

"Gentrified," he agreed, "but in among these there are still plenty of cottages occupied by people who were born on that street, and who've buried grandparents who once lived in their houses. Now where I come from, in Ilford, it's all Indian now, and anyway my own street was only built to house the overflow from East London after the Second World War. You go round to my old house, where I grew up, I mean, enquiring for someone called Curnow, and you'll get nowhere. Here it's different.

"Of course, they've had their fair share of immigrants, and other people from outside, mainly connected with the university, but, as I say, some of the natives are still here." He broke off in wonder. "You know, I talked to one old chap, must have been ninety, and when we'd finished talking he cycled off, scooted along then lifted his leg over the saddle. I won't be able to do that at his age. Sorry, where was I? Yes, he had lived there all his life ..." Michael broke off again. "He still had a lavatory in a little shed at the end of the garden! Even old Nan had inside plumbing!

"But never mind. He remembered Rose Turley because he let her keep her bike chained up in the sideway. Apparently she started life here in lodgings and her landlady wouldn't let her keep her bike in the hall, wanted her to take it round behind and leave it in the shed in the garden, but Rose was afraid someone would steal it, whereas it was safe in this old codger's sideway, because he kept a dog in a kennel in his sideway.

"He told me she didn't stay long, just a couple of years, and then he thought she'd bought her own house on a similar street. The important thing is where she worked. We might have guessed at this — she got a job with the university printers. So I phoned just to see if anyone knew the name and there she was, just like that. Been there all her life."

"You *spoke* to her!"

"The living voice. So tomorrow morning she's staying home and we are going to see her."

"Not 'we', Michael. Me."

All the satisfaction of bearing such good news left his face. He said nothing at first, but picked up his glass and pointed at hers. She shook her head, and he walked to the bar for a refill.

When he returned, he took a large sip and looked across the room, away from her. "What are you up to?" he asked.

"I'm not up to anything. This lady is my client's aunt. My client wants me to see her, and, if possible, re-establish contact. It's personal, Michael. I don't know what to expect."

"Something's fishy."

"There's nothing fishy. I just want to have a private word ..."

"You still think she killed him, don't you? You think he made a pass at her while his wife was in the maternity home and she was disgusted with him and pushed him over the edge. Don't you?"

"I don't think anything of the kind."

"And that the wife knew something like that had happened and told this sister she never wanted to see her again."

"They went up to London together."

"After that, I mean."

"Michael, this is fantastic. Quit it, will you. I don't *know* anything that you don't."

"You think you do, though." Curnow's voice was bleak, betrayed.

"I just want a litle time alone with her. She's of no interest to you or your clients, is she? If I'm alone, I might get a chance to ask her a couple of questions which she *might* answer if no one else is there."

They were interrupted by someone. "Good Lord. Am I not approaching ... the name escapes me but not those lips, those eyes, those teeth, that hair — all in a class beyond compare. Now it comes, Yes! Miss Bramble!"

It was Jim McSweeney from Ward's Island. Lucy was a long time getting his name disentangled from all the others she called up, but eventually it came.

Curnow said, "Here, shove off, you. We're talking."

Lucy said, "We know each other, Michael. Trimble, not Bramble, and I'm surprised to see you, too. On holiday?"

"You must remember. Try," he urged. "Clue: I come to this fair isle for extended periods of time, usually one to two months. I see that you remember. Well done. Now I shan't have to make you write it out a hundred times. What about you? What are you doing here?"

"I'm still involved in the same thing, putting together the story of Greta's birth."

"And have you not yet found the basket in the bullrushes?"

"The what?"

"Moses," Curnow explained, still hostile. "Who *is* this man?"

"I'm sorry: Michael Curnow, Jim McSweeney. Jim was a friend of Greta's mother. Michael is showing me around Cambridge. Let's sit down, shall we?"

"How has Greta's story brought you to Cambridge?" McSweeney asked.

"Greta's aunt lives here. I'm going to see her tomorrow." Lucy checked herself. There was no need, she realized, to let Michael know of McSweeney's presence in Rockingham Cove when Greta was born, or McSweeney of her knowledge of it.

"Ah, so? How have you connected her with the Case of the Mysterious Birth?"

"She was there."

"At the parturition?"

"Yes."

"Greta never knew this. Did she?" He turned to Michael. "I played an avuncular role in the young Greta's life, and I never heard from her of any aunt."

"Greta was shocked when I phoned and told her. Her mother always told her that her aunt simply disappeared, and they never had any contact after that."

"So what do you make of it?"

"I'm guessing that when Greta's mother heard the news as she lay in the maternity home, she got to blaming her sister. Perhaps her husband was afraid of heights, like me. Nothing was said at the inquest. At least, it didn't get into the reported proceedings, did it, Michael?"

"He slipped and fell, Rose Turley said, and that beanpole of a coroner accepted it. Accident. No other cause listed. I doubt if they even took a blood sample, to see if he was drunk. Probably the coroner had a quiet word all round to keep it simple, like he did with that farm worker."

Lucy felt the world unravelling, and tried to pretend the chat was over. "Tomorrow morning I shall meet her."

"What's all this about a farm worker?" McSweeney asked. "I never noticed him in the script."

"There was a farm worker, George Faith, who saw the two walking along the cliff." Lucy tried to be offhand, and continued to gather herself up to leave.

"And what did he see?"

Lucy looked helplessly at Curnow who shrugged. "He saw them kissing and cuddling, he says. Kissing and cuddling."

"And you make nothing of this?" McSweeney said to Lucy.

"The coroner interviewed George Faith before the inquest, and chose not to bring the story out. Quite right, too. He said that the labourer was an old prude who saw what he wanted to see, two Americans up to their usual tricks. I think the coroner was very sensible. The police agreed." And what are you up to? she wondered.

"He told them, did he? Why did he tell you?"

"Because he had heard that I was talking to George Faith, the labourer, and he knew that Faith was still talking about kissing and cuddling to anyone who asked, and though everyone locally had long ago lost interest in what the labourer saw, or made up, the coroner, hearing about us, was afraid that we would be the exception to the rule and rake the whole thing up again."

"And will you?"

"Oh, no."

"Then why don't you go home?" For once, McSweeney spoke without a mask, directly, coolly.

Lucy said, "Because Greta is very excited at the idea of discovering an aunt she had who had disappeared from her life before she was born. I could take back to Greta some idea of how her aunt feels about meeting her. I mean, we don't know why Greta's aunt never came back. If it was something between the two sisters, maybe Greta and her aunt could bury the hatchet, or whatever it is."

"And you, sir?" Some trace of an act had returned to McSweeney as he turned to Curnow.

"I don't know what business it is of yours, but you already heard, I'm showing Mrs. Trimble around."

"But are you not the detective hired by Greta's aunt and uncle on the paternal side to find the evidence to disinherit her?"

"Oh, stop poncing about." Curnow affected a sneering whine. "'*Are you not the detective hired by Lady Rumpole ... ?*' I was, yes, but they're wasting their time. Whoever the natural father may have been, and there's no reason to suppose it wasn't Golden, they were married when Greta was born, so Greta is the heir to anything he had coming. So my job's done. Now it's up to the lawyers. They'll take their time, I don't doubt. And I'll leave when Lucy asks me to and not before. See."

"Oh, Michael, I don't need ... yes, I do. But you can't come with me tomorrow. It might inhibit Greta's aunt. Don't leave yet, though. When I'm done, could we drive out to the coast or something? I've heard a lot about the Norfolk coast. Don't just go away."

Curnow turned to McSweeney. "Satisfied?"

"Replete. I gather you are not looking to swell your company now?"

"No. We're not."

"Michael!" She jumped up and grabbed McSweeney's arm as he went to leave, but he inclined his head and walked away. She turned to Curnow. "He could have joined us for dinner. Now he'll have to eat alone."

"Maybe, But I'll tell you, Lucy, he's up to something, that one. I thought at first he was after you, but now I think he's up to something. I can smell it. What's he doing here?"

"Oh, who cares. A coincidence. He comes to England a lot."

"If I turned up outside your door in Toronto, would you call that a coincidence?"

"It's not the same."

Curnow said, "Well, he's gone now. Let's have another drink and find somewhere to eat. This place would suit me. The roast of the day is leg of lamb. Fancy that again?"

Lucy nodded. Anything. No more than Curnow did she believe that the appearance of McSweeney was a coincidence, but the obvious connection between her search for Greta's roots and McSweeney made her head spin. Besides, except for his height, he did not resemble Greta in any way at all.

After dinner they strolled about the town for an hour, then returned to the lounge for a nightcap, and Curnow explained gently that even the prospect of showing Lucy the fens couldn't keep him from his daughter a day longer than necessary. Lucy had slept so soundly in the afternoon that she was wide awake now, but Curnow was flagging. At eleven, after a second drink, she said, "Bed?" and he opened his eyes and nodded. She said, "You go ahead. I'm going to read for a bit."

When he was out of sight, Lucy went out to the front desk to leave a message for McSweeney. After a brief search, the clerk, as she had suspected he would, said, "There's no one of that name staying here, ma'am." Then she phoned Peter Tse to see if she had any new clients, but he was gone and she left a message on the machine.

Chapter Twenty-three

Colbrooke Road lay on the outside edge of Cambridge, a dead end road, culminating in some college playing fields. Number seventeen was joined to its neighbours on two sides, a tiny former working-class home, at least a hundred years old, Lucy guessed, with a patch of yard in front, and no evident signs of remodelling or renovation, unlike many of its neighbours.

The woman who answered the door looked what she was, a professional in her mid-sixties, dressed in her stay-at-home clothes of sweater and trousers, with a courteous air, and without any wariness or hostility. There was no immediate or striking resemblance to Greta, but nothing in her appearance militated against her being a relation. She was perhaps slightly taller than average, and she probably took a lot of exercise, because she looked the right weight for her height. Her hair which was thick, cut short and springy, might have been a clue, but she had let it go grey, which suited her. Her features were regular, without make-up except for a bit of pink lipstick, and her expression was calm. She could have been any-body's aunt, including Greta's.

Lucy introduced herself.

"I expected you. I took the morning off. I'm Rose Turley," she said. She stood back to let Lucy enter, and led her through the little hall, past the bicycle, into a small dining room at the back of the house. "I'm having the sitting room repainted," she said, "so we have a choice of this or my workroom upstairs. I've crammed a few chairs in here for the moment. I also expected your friend, the man on the phone."

"I asked him to stay away," Lucy said. "I wanted a private word first."

"I'll make some coffee?"

"Please."

Rose Turley disappeared into the kitchen and Lucy sat down and looked around the litle room. The room was packled with the furniture from the sitting room as well as its own; Rose Turley had pushed a round coffee table under the little back window, and arranged three armchairs around it, all facing the win-dow, as a makeshift eating arrangement. This house is about my size, Lucy thought, and then thought how often lately she had been assuming she would ulti-mately be on her own.

Rose returned and sat down. "This is the point at which I am supposed to wonder what this is all about, but of course I've been warned a little by your friend. He told me about your search for information about my niece's birth. How did you find me, by the way?"

"You left behind an address in Cornwall, forty years ago, with the coroner's office. So we knew you had come to Cambridge, and from Greta that you were once a proofreader. So my partner made the obvious phone call and there you were working for the press."

"So you've been down to Rockingham Cove," she said. "Tell me first, why is Greta suddenly so interested in me?"

"Greta has been left some money by an uncle on her father's side."

Rose shook her head several times. "No, no. You are on a fool's errand, I'm afraid. Greta's father was an only child."

Lucy nodded. "He claimed he was, but now it turns out that he had three brothers and two sisters. One of the brothers died recently, and left a lot of money to be shared among the surviving brothers and sisters, or their families. Aubrey didn't tell your sister the truth."

"Well, well. It doesn't surprise me that he was a liar, but why make himself an orphan? Still, I don't see what this has to do with me. What's the problem?"

"It turns out that the other brothers and sisters didn't like Aubrey. They felt he had cut himself off from them and let them down by leaving and not doing his share of caring for the parents in their old age. There must be more to it than that, but that's the story so far."

"Not much they can do about it, though, I would think. The will, I mean."

"That's the point. They think they can do something about it. They claim that Aubrey's child should not benefit from the will because their brother knew that Aubrey was dead, but didn't know that Aubrey had married and had a baby before he died; he didn't intend to leave them anything. They claim he wanted

to leave the money to the surviving siblings that he
knew of. They also claim that since Greta was a
seven-month baby, she might not have been Aubrey's,
that Aubrey might have married June just to legit-
imize the pregnancy. And finally, or finally so far, they
may have medical reasons we don't know about why
Aubrey could not have fathered Greta. They seem to
be hinting at something of the kind. So they are contesting the will to cut Greta out."

"Jarndyce versus Jarndyce."

"What?"

"Nothing. Just muttering. So Greta hired you to
find out ... what?"

"Anything I can. Greta runs a successful business,
and she isn't concerned about the money. I went down
to Rockingham Cove and found out what happened
forty years ago. Something is not quite right. At least
one thing I was able to do was establish that there was
no nonsense of babies being switched in their cradles."
Lucy laughed to show that she thought it sounded
foolish, too. "I made sure Greta was Greta."

"How did you do that?"

"I talked to the midwife, Nanny Barfield, who
told me about Greta's webbed toes."

Rose smiled and raised her eyebrows. "Mrs.
Barfield is still around? My. She must be the last of
her kind, surely. So that's that, then."

"And that was when I heard about you being
there, so I called Greta and she asked me to see if I
could find you. She's intrigued by my discovery of her
aunt. She has no other relatives, as you know, and she
had thought you might be dead."

"But here I am. What can I do for you?"

"Greta doesn't know how her father died. Her mother refused to talk about it. I thought you might tell me how it happened so I could tell her."

"There's the kettle. I'll just be a moment."

"May I use the bathroom while you're gone?"

Rose said, "It's up the stairs to the left."

Lucy climbed the little staircase to the second floor, which consisted of a toilet and separate bathroom at the top of the stairs, and a room at either end. The bathroom was a surprise, intensely feminine in its looks and scents with the slightly antiseptic undersmell which the English seemed to like, compounded of tar soap and Dettol, but along one shelf beside the door lay all the equipment for shaving a beard — brush, razor, soapstick, aftershave lotion — and a leather case to pack it in for travelling.

She took a look through the open bedroom doors, and established that only one of them contained a bed. The other was evidently Rose's workroom.

Downstairs again, a mug of coffee in front of her, Lucy waited for the answer to her request.

"He fell off the cliff," Rose said. "He slipped."

Lucy nodded. "I looked at the spot. Frightening, at least to someone with vertigo."

"I think he must have become dizzy."

"Weren't you by him when he slipped? Didn't you notice anything about him?"

"How do you mean?"

"Did he seem dizzy?"

"I didn't notice at the time, not before he slipped."

"There was a farm labourer, George Faith, who saw you together ..."

"A lot of people saw us together, going for a walk."

"He said you were kissing and cuddling. Those were his words. The coroner chose not to bring that out because it would only cause gossip and might itself be called the same. But I asked him, and the coroner himself confessed he thought that George Faith saw you and Aubrey Golden making love."

"Really? You mean ... ? Standing up?" She laughed. "I had heard about the kissing and cuddling but not about that."

Lucy said, "Where did you hear?"

"Just today. Go on, though. I'll explain in a minute."

"I wondered about the ... er ... love-making, under the circumstances, too. But what *did* Faith see? What happened?"

"Let me think." She sipped her coffee for a few moments. "There was a baby just born," she began, "Aubrey's daughter and my niece. We were both very happy and he probably gave me a kiss. On the cheek. Then he slipped on the wet turf, I grabbed at him— too late — and he fell. That's how it was. That's what the labourer saw."

"What did you do then?"

"I hardly remember. Screamed, I suppose. Then ran back along the cliff to the hotel."

"Did you see a man on a tractor?"

"I didn't see anyone until I ran into the bar."

"Did you run along the path at the edge of the cliff, or the other one, higher up?"

"Just a minute. The path along the cliff. Yes. I just turned and ran, I remember. Why?"

"Did you fall yourself?"

"Yes, I think I did."

"Did you drop anything, an umbrella, something like that?"

"No. What are you going on about?"

"George Faith said you dropped something."

"Did he? Probably my hat. I was wearing a mackintosh sou-wester."

"He picked it up."

"I see." Rose put her cup on the table and composed her skirt before continuing. "And it wasn't a hat?"

"It was a pack of American Express travellers' cheques."

"Oh, yes, I remember now," Rose said, after a pause, speaking woodenly. "That's right. Travellers' cheques."

It wasn't this single clue that revealed the truth. Slowly all the mysteries came together: why Greta's mother had kept away from old friends after Greta's birth; why Rose had never returned; and even, perhaps, what Jim McSweeney was doing in Cambridge at this moment. It just needed to be said.

Gently, Lucy asked, "Why would someone living in England be carrying travellers' cheques to go on holiday in England? And George Faith found them on the road, not on the path. He said you ran up to the road before you turned for the inn." She waited politely before continuing. "It wasn't you on the cliff, was it?"

Rose seemed to relax. Eventually she shook her head. "No."

"You are Greta's mother, aren't you?"

Rose leaned back in her chair, drew up her knees and put her arms around them, in a gesture that now reminded Lucy sharply of Greta. "How melodramatic that sounds," Rose said. "Yes, I am Greta's mother."

"And it was Greta's legal mother who walked along the cliff with her husband."

The woman nodded slightly.

"Then who is Greta's father?"

"That's not really any of your business, is it?"

"It's Greta's business. I have to tell her that I at least asked you."

Rose hugged herself and looked out the window at the little garden. "The chrysanthemums will be good this year," she said. "Why don't I make some more coffee and take the telephone off the hook and tell you a story. Shall I? Then you can decide what to do with it. I don't think you will do much."

Lucy waited in silence as Rose uncoiled herself and moved into the kitchen. She talked through the doorway while she made the coffee. "I've been waiting forty years for someone like you to come along, though after the first couple of years I stopped being apprehensive. You've done well. Clever."

"It was the travellers' cheques that clued me in. Nothing much. But when I realized whose cheques they were, I got the mad idea that someone might be impersonating her sister. It was easy to trip you up once I had George Faith's story in my head."

"No one noticed at the time, so I thought we'd got away with it." She came through the door and poured out the coffee, then rearranged herself in the arm-chair. "I'll tell you the whole story, then we can talk about it."

Lucy watched her for signs of artifice or hesitation, but she had a truthful air.

Rose continued. "In the winter of 1957, I got into a bitter fight with my mother because I wanted to move

out and live on my own, or with another girl. I was at
the University of Manitoba and living at home, and my
mother suspected I wanted to sleep with boys. That
was true, we all did, wanted to sleep with boys, I mean,
but mostly I just wanted to get away from her. I still
don't have any fond memories of her, but that's neither
here nor there. In the end, I realized that if I wanted my
own life I would have to leave Winnipeg, so I did. I left
Winnipeg and moved to Toronto to be near June in
case I needed someone. I'll abbreviate the next bit. I *did*
get into trouble and June looked after me. In the spring,
I got pregnant. I was distraught. I couldn't go back to
Winnipeg — my mother would have taken me in, she
wasn't that bad, but the price would have been too
high. Unmarried mothers were rare then, and I had to
find somewhere where no one knew me, have the baby,
and put it up for adoption. What nice girls from Winnipeg did in those days was 'take a trip' to England."

"Was an abortion not possible?"

"It was hard to arrange in '57, if you were
healthy. I didn't like the idea myself, and June argued
furiously against it, offering to give me all the help
she could if I had the baby. So she scraped up some
money, and I moved to England. I was something of
an anglophile already."

"Did you manage to keep it secret?"

"From everyone in Canada except for June, and
one other person. Not the father, I have to tell you."
She stretched out her legs and put her hands behind
her head. "I'm enjoying this," she said suddenly,
and held up her hand to prevent Lucy interrupting
yet. "Thus it came to pass that I had hardly found
myself a room in Cambridge — I've always lived

here — than I got a letter from June. She was getting married, and, to cut to the chase, she told me
she was barren, that Aubrey knew and didn't care,
and they wanted to adopt my baby when it came.
So we concocted the little scheme you've uncovered,
which was incredibly easy, and I had come to
believe was flawless, until you came along. At any
rate, it worked. So there it is. I am Greta's mother,
but she had a good substitute, didn't she?"

"You've never gone back to see Greta?"

"No, June was quite firm about that."

"Why?"

"She was concerned that I would start yearning to
know the child in a few years ..." the woman spoke
lightly, but the intention was serious "... as indeed I did,
and perhaps somehow it would show and the child or
someone would guess. At the time it didn't seem such a
hard decision. I didn't feel very maternal, just 'caught,'
as we used to say. Then my sister learned that she could-
n't conceive. Unlike me then, she was maternal by
instinct, so we made some kind of match. There was
nothing to it. She faked a pregnancy and she and
Aubrey came over early enough to fake a premature
birth, and she and I simply registered and lived as each
other for two weeks. It didn't even seem illegal."

"It might have made a difference at the inquest if
the coroner had known."

"Possibly."

"On the other hand, the kissing and cuddling on
the cliff makes a new kind of sense. Perfectly natural
between husband and wife."

"They weren't cuddling. More like struggling, I
would think. I can tell you now, since it's unprovable,

and you are a sensible person who will see the need to keep it to yourself, that Rose killed her husband."

"Did she tell you?"

"Yes."

"Why? though I'm beginning to have an idea."

A key turned in the lock and the front door opened. Jim McSweeney walked in, nodded agreeably to Lucy, kissed Rose, and said, "Any coffee left?" and sat in the third chair, so that they formed a semi-circle facing the window. "Like the front row of the dress circle," McSweeney said.

Lucy's eyes swung back and forth between the two lovers, getting now the answer to her question. She turned to Rose. "You two talked to each other this morning. You knew what I was going to say before I came, didn't you?"

"Not all of it. Just what you told Jim in the hotel last night."

Lucy looked at McSweeney. "Tell me, are you Greta's father?"

McSweeney arranged himself in his chair, accepted his coffee from Rose, sipped, and said, "I wish it were so. But no."

"But you two are ..." She waved a finger between them.

"Bespoke? An item? Yes, indeed. I told you I come to England several times a year for several weeks at a time. I come here. I am Rose's fancy man, am I not, my dear, have been since time eternal. Though circumstances keep us apart much of the time. I am also the go-between. I bring news of Greta to Rose, and I used to take news of Rose to June, and, a long time ago, money from June to Rose. But it is true that this time I knew I would find you here. Greta telephoned me and brought me up to date on your quest. I realized immediately that the game was up and I left on the midnight packet, carrying only a change of linen and my trusty pistol, and this." He held out a photograph to Rose. "You remember? Taken just before you left Toronto. I found it among some memorabilia."

"I had a bun. I'd forgotten." Rose looked at the picture in delight, as McSweeney watched her, fondly.

"Oh, goddamn you two," Lucy cried. "What's going on?"

"We are being rude," McSweeney said immediately. "Here's how it is. I fell in love with this lady in 1957, but she was already pregnant, knew it, didn't want me to know it, and gallantly — can that word be declined in the female case? — ran away. She was right to do so. In 1957 I was not mature (he pronounced the word with an American accent — 'matoor'); me poisonality hadn't developed enough to marry someone bearing another's child."

"Was it the fat professor you caught her with at the party?"

Rose spoke. "Poor Derek. He never assaulted me. I was drunk, and he came in and tried to tidy me up."

"Then *who* jumped you for God's sake? The book dealer?"

Rose shook her head. "There aren't many left, are there?"

"Good God," Lucy said. "Aubrey Golden."

"Now you know it all."

Lucy began to laugh. "So Aubrey was Greta's father?"

"No one else found it funny," Rose said. "That's why my sister pushed him off the cliff. He told her while they were out on the walk. I think he had the idea that she would be pleased that 'her' child would at least have him as a father. But she was so — what? — sickened? — that she pushed him off the cliff and came back to me that night to confirm the story he had told her. She was still in a state. I calmed her down, told her she didn't really kill him, just wanted to, and that I would have had no part of Aubrey. He had seduced me earlier, actually more of a rape than a seduction, and I wasn't sorry he was dead. And why should that change the plan? She wanted a baby, I didn't. So I handed Greta over at London Airport, and never saw her again. What's so funny?"

Lucy, slightly hysterical, told them about Michael Curnow. "They have been trying to question Greta's legitimacy as Golden's heir. If their lawyer finds out about this he will have a ball. But they won't, will they? Greta is Golden's daughter, never mind all the rest. I won't tell Michael and you two won't tell anyone else."

Then, calming down, she said, "I'm still not quite sure why June cut herself off from her old friends, but I'm beginning to see ..."

"It was the easiest way, she said. She'd managed to fake a pregnancy — Mother Hubbard dresses, that kind of thing. Then she went to England and came back with a baby that her old crowd would know was premature. So she dropped her old crowd before anyone got a good look in the cradle. It worked. After six months you would have needed to be a pediatrician to see a two-month difference in Greta's growth.

"We talked about it, chiefly through Jim. She saw it as the simplest way to avoid questions which would get her tangled up in a lot of little lies. She could be quite ruthless, my sister, but I was the only one who suffered, and I still think, on the whole, given the times and all that there, that it was for the best. Then.

"I never went back to Toronto, and I never saw Greta again. June and I met every time she came near Cambridge on a buying trip, about every two or three years, and I did go back to Winnipeg once, when our mother died — June didn't — but that was the only time. By then I'd lost touch with anyone I knew there."

"Was there an estate?"

"Did my mother leave anything? A few thousand dollars and the house. She left it all to me. I asked June if she wanted her share, but she wouldn't hear of it." They sat in silence for a few minutes, then Rose said, "What now?"

Lucy said, "Are you going to get in touch with Greta?"

"I want to. Do you think she will?"

"Want to? That's why I'm here. Call her today."

Rose shook her head. "What I'd like is for you to go home first and tell her the whole story. Then call me. *Then* I'll call her. I want to be sure that I'm ... welcome."

Lucy reported to Michael at the hotel. "I'm glad I met Greta's aunt," she said. "I persuaded her to meet her niece again."

"Bugger Greta's aunt. I want to know about you. Will I ever see you again?"

"Don't say it like that. Of course you will."

And then she saw Greta Golden appear in the doorway, recognize her, and start to cross the room. She put her arms around Michael and held up a flat palm behind his back to warn Greta off. "Give me a kiss, Michael."

He muzzled her face for a moment, said, "Ah, well," and picked up his bag. "By the way I'm not a complete bloody fool," he said. "Old Nan told me the truth. That baby wasn't premature; a week or two late, if anything. Weighed nine pounds. Greta's mother wouldn't have been allowed on a plane in that condition. Another thing, I heard this morning from my client that my job's finished, yours too, I would think, in one respect. Apparently the income tax boys have laid claim to Geoffrey's estate on the grounds that he never paid any tax last year or the year before that — it goes back a long way — and they are going to hang on to it until the police have had time to prove he got most of the money illegally. The solicitors no longer have access to any money except their own, so they've laid themselves off and me, too. Ah, well. No skin off our nose, is it? Ta-ta." He went through the door that had just opened on Greta.

"Who was that?" Greta asked.

Lucy said, "A new friend, I hope. Now, what are you doing here? How did you know where I was? The hotel, I mean."

"I called your landlord. Before I forget, he gave me a message for you. Here it is, 'But the next day, when they opened the trunk, the body was gone.' You know what that means?"

"Yes. It always is." Lucy smiled, clenching her fists and raising her arms, her life returning to normal. "Now it's your turn."

She waited for more, then shrugged. "None of my business, eh? Me, now. I have the most extraordinary news. I found someone who remembered the name of mother's doctor. First of all, our blood groups match, but look at this." She thrust a letter into Lucy's hand. It was from a Toronto gynecologist to a general practitioner, dated May 15, 1957. Much of it was incomprehensible, but a phrase at the end, "there is no possibility of conception," said it all.

Lucy said, "I think I know ..."

Greta held up her hand. "Let me tell you the whole story first. I called my doctor and read the letter to her and she said the reason was that Mother had once had a botched abortion. *That's* probably why her own mother disowned her, or the other way round. Apparently Mama perpetrated a giant hoax on my father. She arranged somehow to adopt a baby and have me registered in her name. I doubt if Aubrey knew she was barren — isn't that a magnificent word? — bleak and terrifying, of course, but huge and biblical — or he would never have married her, would he? The upshot of it all was that now I don't know who my mother was, let alone my father. What do you think I should do?"

"Put the letter in your safety deposit box and forget about it. Did the records show anything about Aubrey?"

"Nothing. Nothing at all. Just that he didn't have pox."

"Then put the letter away. Let me tell you the rest of the story. I saw Rose Turley today, your mother's

269 and then Lucy

sister. I'll take you to her tomorrow." And then Lucy told her the real story.

The next evening, after a day of bringing together mother and daughter, and delivering Greta to Colbrooke Road, then getting a call saying that Greta was going to spend the evening with Rose, Lucy went into the bar after dinner for a peaceful coffee, wondering if Greta had discovered a new aunt, or a new mother, and realizing that the stability of everyone's world, even without the legacy, depended on Rose remaining an aunt. The barman interrupted her thoughts to say that someone had been enquiring after her earlier in the evening. "He wouldn't leave his name, ma'am. Just said to say he'd be here after the races. Newmarket, I would think he meant."

So he had come, after all. Lucy picked up her purse. "When he comes back, if he does, would you tell him that I've gone?"

The barman looked unhappy. "He could check at the desk, ma'am, see if you're still registered. I'd wind up in the middle."

Lucy thought of a good revision. "Then would you tell him that I told you to say that I was gone? Just like that. Say 'She told me to tell you that she was gone.' Wink, if you like. Then you'll be off the hook."

"Why don't you tell him yourself?"

She stared at the door into the other bar where the voice came from and there, walking towards her was the Trog, Ben Nolan, in all his shiny-pated, gap-toothed glory.

He perched on the arm of the chair facing her. "I happened to be talking to Peter Tse out at the track," he said, "And he told me you were here. I've just come over to spend a few days at the races. Off to Ireland tomorrow. Want to come? There's room."

"Oh, yes," she said immediately, responding to the flood of agreeableness that was replacing the apprehension that had possessed her. "Oh, yes, but I can't. I have to go back to Toronto first and sort something out." She paused. "Me," she added.

He looked around the room, then at his watch. "I just stopped off here just in case you were around. Thought I would say hello. I've got a message for you, by the way, from your landlord. He said the drugstore guy sent you some flowers. Another conquest, Lucy?"

Lucy laughed. "A grateful client. How many of you are there here?"

Now he slid down into the seat, reached over, and took her hand. "There's just me, Lucy. I came over by myself. I could stay if you want. We could have a drink."

She withdrew her hand. "Still telling lies?"

"Only in a good cause, Lucy. Same as ever. You?"

"Have you seen Johnny lately?" she asked, reminding him of her status, still intact as far as the world was concerned.

"Comstock? Yeah, I saw him, too, at Woodbine. But I didn't speak to him. He was busy, getting a horse ready for the race."

Something in his voice made her ask. "Was he by himself?"

"There's always a lot of people round the barns."

"But was there anyone with him?"

"There's been someone tagging around for a while, Lucy. That's why I came. I thought you and Comstock were history, maybe. Thought you could use an old friend."

In public, too, she thought. I'm the last person to know. Classical. This growing up in leaps and bounds was exhausting. But there was pride involved yet. "You've got a nerve, presuming like that," she said.

"I know. But who were you telling to get lost when I came in? It wasn't me, was it? You didn't know I was here. Who did you think left a message for you?"

Lucy gave up, putting her hand over his, slightly overcome by the realization that he had flown the Atlantic in pursuit of her. "Never mind. You're here now. Yes, you can buy me a drink. Make it a double. Toronto can wait."